THE DIMITRAKOS
PROPOSITION

D0500104

THE DIMITRAKOS PROPOSITION

BY

LYNNE GRAHAM

All rights reserved including the right of reproduction in whole or in part in any form. This edition is published by arrangement with Harlequin Books S.A.

This is a work of fiction. Names, characters, places, locations and incidents are purely fictional and bear no relationship to any real life individuals, living or dead, or to any actual places, business establishments, locations, events or incidents. Any resemblance is entirely coincidental.

This book is sold subject to the condition that it shall not, by way of trade or otherwise, be lent, resold, hired out or otherwise circulated without the prior consent of the publisher in any form of binding or cover other than that in which it is published and without a similar condition including this condition being imposed on the subsequent purchaser.

® and TM are trademarks owned and used by the trademark owner and/or its licensee. Trademarks marked with ® are registered with the United Kingdom Patent Office and/or the Office for Harmonisation in the Internal Market and in other countries.

First published in Great Britain 2014
by Mills & Boon, an imprint of Harlequin (UK) Limited,
Large Print edition 2014
Eton House, 18-24 Paradise Road,
Richmond, Surrey, TW9 1SR

© 2014 Lynne Graham

ISBN: 978 0 263 24048 1

Harlequin (UK) Limited's policy is to use papers that are natural, renewable and recyclable products and made from wood grown in sustainable forests. The logging and manufacturing processes conform to the legal environmental regulations of the country of origin.

Printed and bound in Great Britain
by CPI Antony Rowe, Chippenham, Wiltshire

CHAPTER ONE

'BEARING IN MIND the history of the company's expansion and success, it *is* a most unjust will,' Stevos Vannou, Ash's lawyer, declared heavily in the simmering silence, a wary eye locked to the very tall, dark and powerfully built male across the office.

Acheron Dimitrakos, known as Ash to his inner circle, and Greek billionaire founder of the global giant DT Industries, said nothing. He did not trust himself to speak. Usually his control was absolute. But not today. He had trusted his father, Angelos, as far as he trusted anyone, which was to say *not* very much, but it had never once crossed his mind that the older man would even consider threatening the company that Ash had single-handedly built with the bombshell that his last will and testament had become. If Ash didn't marry within the year, he would lose half of the company to his stepmother and her children, who were already most amply provided for by the terms of his father's will. It was unthinkable; it was a brutally unfair demand, which ran contrary to every honourable scruple and the high standards that Ash had once believed the older man held dear to his heart. It just went to show— as if Ash had ever had any doubt—you couldn't trust anybody, and your nearest and dearest were the most likely to plunge a knife into your back when you were least expecting it.

'DT is *my* company,' Ash asserted between compressed lips.

'But regretfully not on paper,' Stevos countered gravely. 'On paper you never had your father transfer his interest to you. Even though it is indisputably the company that *you* built.'

Still, Ash said nothing. Cold dark eyes fringed with ridiculously long black lashes locked on the sweeping view of the City of London skyline that his penthouse office enjoyed, his lean, darkly handsome features set in hard, forbidding lines of restraint. 'A long court case disputing the will would seriously undermine the company's ability to trade,' he said eventually.

'Picking a wife would definitely be the lesser evil,' the lawyer suggested with a cynical chuckle. 'That's all you have to do to put everything back to normal.'

'My father knew I had no intention of ever marrying. That is exactly why he did this to me,' Ash ground out between clenched teeth, his temper momentarily escaping its leash as he thought of the utterly unhinged woman his misguided father had expected him to put in the role. 'I don't want a wife. I don't want children. I don't want *any* of that messing up my life!'

Stevos Vannou cleared his throat and treated his employer to a troubled appraisal. He had never seen Acheron Dimitrakos betray anger before or, indeed, any kind of emotion. The billionaire head of DT Industries was usually as cold as ice, possibly even colder, if his discarded lovers in the many tabloid stories were to be believed. His cool, logical approach, his reserve and lack of human sentiment were the stuff of legend. According to popular repute when one of his PAs had gone into labour at a board summit, he had told her to stay and finish the meeting.

'Forgive me if I'm being obtuse but I would suggest that any number of women would line up to marry you,' Ash's companion remarked cautiously, thinking of his own wife, who threatened to swoon if she even saw Acheron's face in print. 'Choosing would be more of a challenge than actually finding a wife.'

Ash clamped his mouth shut on an acid rejoinder, well aware the portly little Greek was out of his depth and only trying to be helpful even if stating the obvious was more than a little simplistic. He knew he could snap his fingers and get a wife as quickly and easily as he could get a woman into his bed. And he understood exactly why it was *so* easy: the money was the draw. He had a fleet of private jets and homes all over the world, not to mention servants who waited on him and his guests hand and foot. He paid well for good service. He was a generous lover too but every time he saw dollar signs in a woman's eyes it turned him off hard and fast. And more and more he noticed the dollar signs *before* he noticed the beautiful body and that was taking sex off the menu more often than he liked. He needed sex as he needed air to breathe, and couldn't really comprehend why he found the greed and manipulation that went with it so profoundly repellent. Evidently somewhere down inside him, buried so deep he couldn't root it out, there lurked an over-sensitive streak he despised.

It was worse that Acheron knew exactly what lay behind the will and he could only marvel at his father's inability to appreciate that the woman he had tried to push Acheron towards was anathema to him. Six months before the older man's death there had been a big scene at his father's home, and Acheron had steered clear of visiting since then, which was simply one more nail in the coffin of the proposed bride-to-be. He had tried to talk to his stepmother about the problem but nobody had been willing to listen to common sense, least of all his father, who had been sufficiently impressed by the lady's acting ability to decide that the young woman he had raised from childhood would make his only son the perfect wife.

'Of course, perhaps it is possible that you could simply ignore the will and *buy* out your stepmother's interest in the company,' the lawyer suggested glibly.

Unimpressed, Ash shot the older man a sardonic glance. 'I will not pay for what is mine by right. Thank you for your time.'

Recognising the unmistakable note of dismissal, Stevos hastily stood up to leave while resolving to inform his colleagues of the situation immediately to sort out a plan of action. 'I'll put the best business minds in the firm on this challenge.'

Jaw line clenched as hard as a rock, Ash nodded even though he had little hope of a rescue plan. Experience told him that his father would have taken legal advice as well and would never have placed such a binding clause in his will without the assurance that it was virtually foolproof.

A wife, Ash reflected grimly. He had known since childhood that he would never take a wife and never father a child. That caring, loving gene had passed him by. He had no desire for anyone to grow up in his image or follow in his footsteps, nor did he wish to pass on the darkness he kept locked up inside himself. In fact, he didn't even like children, what little contact he had had with them simply bearing out his belief that children were noisy, difficult and annoying. Why would any sane adult want something that had to be looked after twenty-four hours a day and gave you sleepless nights into the bargain? In the same way why would any man want only one woman in his bed? The *same* woman, night after night, week after week. Ash shuddered at the very suggestion of such severe sexual confinement.

He recognised that he had a decision to make and he resolved to act fast before the news of that ridiculous will hit the marketplace and damaged the company he had built his life around.

'Nobody sees Mr Dimitrakos without an appointment *and* his prior agreement,' the svelte receptionist repeated frigidly. 'If you don't leave, Miss Glover, I will be forced to call Security to have you removed from the building.'

In answer, Tabby plonked her slight body back down on the plush seating in the reception area. Across from her sat an older man studying documents from a briefcase and talking urgently in a foreign language on his cell phone. Knowing she looked like hell did nothing for her confidence in such luxurious surroundings but she hadn't had a full night's sleep for some time, she no longer owned any decent clothes and she was desperate. Nothing *less* than desperation would have brought her to DT Industries seeking an interview with the absolute seven-letter-word of a man who had summarily refused to take any responsibility for the child whom Tabby loved with all her heart. Acheron Dimitrakos was a selfish, arrogant pig and what she had read about his womanising exploits in one of her clients' glossy scandal-sheet magazines had not improved her opinion. The man who had more money than Midas had turned his back on Amber without even expressing a desire to meet with Tabby as his co-guardian, or checking out the little girl's welfare.

The call to Security by Reception was duly made in clear crystalline tones undoubtedly intended to scare Tabby off before the guards arrived. Her small face stiff, she stayed where she was, her slight body rigid with tension while she frantically tried to think up another plan of approach because gatecrashing Acheron's office wasn't going very well. But it wasn't as if she had had a choice, although she acknowledged that the situation was very serious indeed when such a callous personality became her last hope.

And then fate took a hand she wasn't expecting and she wasted a split second simply staring when she saw the tall dark man from the magazine pictures striding across Reception with a couple of suited men following in his wake. Tabby flew to her feet and raced after him. 'Mr Didmitrakos… Mr Dimitrakos!' she launched, stumbling over the syllables of his wretchedly complicated surname.

And at the exact same moment as her very tall and commanding quarry paused by the lift wearing an expression of sheer disbelief at her approach, the security guards came at a literal run, muttering fervent apologies to the man in front of her!

'I'm Amber's other guardian, Tabby Glover!' Tabby explained in feverish haste as both her arms were suddenly grabbed by the two men with him and she was yanked back a step from her proximity to him. 'I need to see you…I tried to get an appointment but I couldn't even though it's desperately important that we talk before the weekend!'

Security really was in need of sharpening up if they allowed him to be cornered on the top floor of his own building by a crazy woman, Ash reflected in exasperation. The young woman was wearing a worn jacket, track pants and trainers, her fair hair tied up in a high ponytail, pale shadowed face bare of make-up. She was small and plain, not at all the kind of woman who would have attracted his attention…although no sooner had he decided that than he noticed her remarkable blue eyes, which were an unusual violet in shade and dominated her pinched features.

'Please!' Tabby gasped. 'You can't be this selfish—nobody could be! Amber's father was a member of your family—'

'I have no family,' Ash informed her drily. 'Escort her out,' he told the security officers, who took over from his bodyguards in restraining Tabby even though she hadn't put up a struggle. 'And make sure this doesn't happen again.'

Taken aback that he wouldn't even give her five

minutes of his time, that he betrayed no recognition even of Amber's name, Tabby was momentarily silenced. Then she swore at him like a fishwife, angrily employing language that had never left her lips before. In response, his brilliant dark eyes glittered with a raw angry hostility that momentarily shocked her because that cool front he wore evidently concealed much murkier depths.

'Mr Dimitrakos…?' Another voice interposed, and Tabby turned her head in surprise to see the older man who had been seated near her in the waiting area.

'The child—you'll recall your late cousin's guardianship request, which you turned down a couple of months ago?' Stevos Vannou hurtled forward to remind Acheron Dimitrakos in a quiet, respectful undertone.

An inconsequential memory pinged in the back of Ash's shrewd brain and drew his straight black brows together into a frown. 'What of it?'

'You selfish bastard!' Tabby raked at him, outraged by his lack of reaction and the consequences that his indifference to Amber's fate were about to visit on the child. 'I'll go to the press with this…you don't deserve anything better. All that wretched money and you can't do anything good with it!'

'*Siopi!* Keep quiet,' Acheron told her sternly in Greek and then English.

'And you and whose army is going to make me?' Tabby snapped back, unimpressed, the fighting spirit that had carried her through many years of loss and disappointment rising to the fore again to strengthen her backbone.

'What does she want?' Acheron asked his lawyer in English as if she weren't there.

'I suggest we take this back into your office,' Stevos remarked on a loaded hint.

Savage impatience gripped Ash. Only three days earlier he had returned from his father's funeral and, without even allowing for his grief at the older man's sudden death from a heart attack, it had turned into a very frustrating week. The very last thing he was in the mood for was a drama about some child he had never met and couldn't have cared less about. Troy Valtinos, oh, yes, he could remember now, a third cousin he had also *never* met, who had unexpectedly died and, in doing so, had attempted to commit his infant daughter to Ash's care. An act of sheer inexplicable insanity, Acheron reflected in exasperation, thinking back incredulously to that brief discussion with Stevos some months earlier. He was a childless single male without family back-up and he travelled constantly. What on earth could anyone have supposed he would do with an orphaned baby girl?

'I'm sorry I swore at you,' Tabby lied valiantly in an effort to build a bridge and win a hearing. 'I shouldn't have done that—'

'Your mouth belongs in the gutter,' Acheron breathed icily and he addressed the security guards, 'Free her. You can take her out when I'm done with her.'

Tabby gritted her teeth together, straightened her jacket and ran uncertain hands down over her slender denim-clad thighs. Ash briefly studied her oval face, his attention lingering on her full pink mouth as a rare flight of sexual fantasy took him to the brink of picturing where else that mouth might be best employed other than in the gutter. The stirring at his groin put him in an even worse mood, reminding him of how long it had been since he had indulged his healthy libido. He knew he had to be in a very bad way if he could react to such an ignorant female.

'I'll give you five minutes of my valuable time,' Acheron breathed with chilling reluctance.

'Five minutes when a child's life and happiness hang in the balance? How very generous of you,' Tabby replied sarcastically.

Roaring rancour assailed Acheron because he wasn't accustomed to such rudeness, particularly not from women. 'You're insolent as well as vulgar.'

'It got me in the door, didn't it? Politeness got me nowhere,' Tabby traded, thinking of the many phone calls she had made in vain requests for an appointment. As for being called cheeky and vulgar, did she really care what some jumped-up, spoilt snob with loads of money thought about her? Yet her brain was already scolding her for her aggressive approach, telling her it was unwise. If she could get around the freeze front Acheron Dimitrakos wore to the world, he was in a position to help Amber while she was not. As far as Social Services were concerned, she could not be considered a suitable guardian for Amber because she was single, had no decent home and was virtually penniless.

'Start talking,' Ash urged, thrusting the door of his office shut.

'I need your help to keep Amber in my custody. I'm the only mother she's ever known and she's very attached to me. Social Services are planning to take her off me on Friday and place her in foster care with a view to having her adopted.'

'Isn't that the best plan in the circumstances?' Ash's lawyer, Stevos Vannou, interposed in a very reasonable voice as though it was an expected thing that she should be willing to surrender the child she loved. 'I seem to remember that you are single and living on benefits and that a child would be a considerable burden for you—'

Acheron had frozen the instant the phrase 'foster care' came his way but neither of his companions had noticed. It was a closely guarded secret that Ash, in spite of the fact his mother had been one of the richest Greek heiresses ever born, had once spent years of his life in foster care, shifted from home to home, family to family, enduring everything from genuine care to indifference to outright cruelty and abuse. And he had never, ever forgotten the experience.

'I haven't lived on benefits since Amber's mother, Sonia, passed away. I looked after Sonia until she died and that was why I couldn't work,' Tabby protested, and shot a glance brimming with offended pride at Acheron's still figure. 'Look, I'm not just some freeloader. A year ago Sonia and I owned our own business and it was thriving until Troy died and she fell ill. In the fall-out, I lost everything as well. Amber is the most important thing in my world but, in spite of me being chosen as one of her guardians, there's no blood tie between Amber and me and that gives me very little real claim to her in law.'

'Why have you come to me?' Ash enquired drily.

Tabby rolled her eyes, helplessly inflamed by his attitude. 'Troy thought you were such a great guy—'

Ash tensed, telling himself that none of what

she had told him was any of his business, yet the thought of an innocent baby going into foster care roused a riot of reactions inside him drawn from his own memories. 'But I never met Troy.'

'He did *try* to meet you because he said his mother, Olympia, used to work for your mother,' Tabby recounted.

Acheron suddenly frowned, straight black brows pleating as old memories stirred. Olympia Carolis, he recalled very well as having been one of his mother's carers. He had not appreciated when the guardianship issue had arisen that Troy was Olympia's son because he had only known her by her name before marriage, although if he stretched his memory to the limit he could vaguely recall that she had been expecting a child when she left his mother's employ. That child could only have been Troy.

'Troy was frantic to find a job here in London and you were his business idol,' Tabby told him curtly.

'His...*what*?' Ash repeated with derision.

'False flattery won't advance your cause,' Stevos Vannou declared, much more at home in the current meeting than he had been in the last, for the matter of the will would require considerable research of case law to handle.

'It wasn't false or flattery,' Tabby contradicted sharply, angry with the solicitor for taking that attitude and switching her attention back to Ash. 'It was the truth. Troy admired your business achievements very much. He even took the same business degree you did. That and the fact he saw you as head of his family explains why he put you down as a guardian in his will.'

'And there was I, innocent that I am, thinking it was only because I was rich,' Acheron breathed with sardonic bite, his dark deep drawl vibrating down her spine.

'You really are a hateful, unfeeling creep!' Tabby slammed back at him tempestuously, fiery emotion ablaze in her violet eyes. 'Troy was a lovely man. Do you honestly think he realised that he was going to die at the age of twenty-four in a car accident? Or that his wife would suffer a stroke within hours of giving birth? Troy would never have taken a penny from anyone that he hadn't earned first.'

'Yet this lovely man left both his widow and child destitute,' Ash reminded her censoriously.

'He didn't have a job, and Sonia was earning enough money at the time through the business we owned. Neither of them could possibly have foreseen that both of them would be dead within a year of having that will drawn up.'

'But it was scarcely fair to name me as a guardian without prior discussion of the idea,' Acheron pointed out drily. 'The normal thing to do would have been to ask my permission first.'

Rigid with tension, Tabby made no comment. She recognised that he had a point but refused to acknowledge the direct hit.

'Perhaps you could tell us without further waste of time exactly what you imagine Mr Dimitrakos could do to help you?' Stevos Vannou sliced in, standing on the sidelines and thoroughly disconcerted by the sheer level of biting hostility erupting between his usually imperturbable employer and his visitor.

'I want to ask Mr Dimitrakos to support my wish to adopt Amber.'

'But is that a realistic goal, Miss Glover?' the

lawyer countered immediately. 'You have no home, no money and no partner, and my own experience with Social Services and child-custody cases tells me that at the very least you need a stable lifestyle to be considered a suitable applicant to adopt.'

'What the heck does having or not having a partner have to do with it?' Tabby demanded defensively. 'This past year I've been far too busy to waste time looking for a man.'

'And with your approach it might have proved a considerable challenge,' Acheron interposed without hesitation.

Tabby opened and closed her lush mouth in angry disconcertion and took a seething step closer to the Greek billionaire. 'You accused me of having no manners? What about your own?' she snapped in outrage.

Studying the two adults before him squabbling and insulting each other much as his own teenaged children did, Stevos averted his attention from them both. 'Miss Glover? If you had had a partner it would certainly have made a big difference to your application. Raising a child today is a challenge and it is widely believed that *two* parents generally make that easier.'

'Well, unfortunately for me a partner isn't something I can dig up overnight!' Tabby exclaimed, wishing the wretched man would think of something other than picking holes in her suitability to adopt Amber. Didn't she have enough to worry about?

A germ of a wild idea leapt into Stevos's brain, and he skimmed his insightful gaze to Acheron and addressed him in Greek. 'You know, you could both help each other...'

Ash frowned. 'In what possible way?'

'She needs a stable home and partner to support her adoption application—you need a wife. With a little compromise on both sides and some serious legal negotiation, you could both achieve what you want and nobody would ever need to know the truth.'

Acheron was always quick on the uptake but for a split second he literally could not believe that Stevos had made that speech, could even have *dared* to suggest such an insane idea. He shot a disdainful glance at Tabby Glover and all her many obvious deficiencies and his black brows went skyward. 'You *have* to be out of your mind,' he told his lawyer with incredulity. 'She's a foul-mouthed girl from the back streets!'

'You've got the money to clean her up enough to pass in public,' the older man replied drily. 'I'm talking about a wife you *pay* to be your wife, not a normal wife. If you get married, *all* your problems with regard to ownership of the company go away—'

In brooding silence, Acheron focused on the one massive problem that would not go away in that scenario—Tabby Glover. *Not wife material* screeched every one of his sophisticated expectations, but he was also thinking about what he had learned about Troy Valtinos and his late mother, Olympia, and his conscience was bothering him on that score. 'I couldn't marry her. I don't like her—'

'Do you *need* to like her?' Stevos enquired quietly. 'I shouldn't have thought that was a basic requirement to meet the terms of a legal stipulation to protect your company. You own many properties. I'm sure you could put her in one of them and barely notice she was there.'

'Right at this moment the first thing on my agenda has to be the child,' Acheron startled his lawyer by asserting. 'I want to check up on her. I have been remiss in my responsibilities and too quick to dismiss them.'

'Look…' While Stevos was engaged in giving Ash an alarmed look at that sudden uncharacteristic swerve of his into child-welfare territory, Tabby had folded her arms in frustration and she was glowering at the two men. 'If you two are going to keep on chatting in a foreign language and acting like I'm not here—'

'If only you were not,' Ash murmured silkily.

Tabby's hands balled into fists. 'I bet quite a few women have thumped you in your time!'

Shimmering eyes dark as sloes challenged her, his lean strong face slashing into a sudden smile of raw amusement. 'Not a one…'

Amber, Tabby reminded herself with painful impact, her heart clenching at the thought of the child she adored. She was here to ask for his help for Amber's sake, and Amber's needs were the

most important consideration, not how objection-
able she found the despicable man. His charismatic smile struck her like a deluge of icy water.
He was incredibly, really quite breathtakingly,
handsome and the fact that he found her amusing hurt. Of course, Tabby had never cherished
many illusions about her desirability factor as a
woman. Although she had always had a lot of
male friends, she'd had very few boyfriends, and
Sonia had once tactfully tried to hint that Tabby
could be too sharp-tongued, too independent and
too critical to appeal to the average male. Unfortunately, nobody had ever explained to Tabby
how she could possibly have survived her challenging life without acquiring those seemingly
unfeminine attributes.

'You want to meet the child?' Stevos stepped in
quickly before war broke out again between his
companions and wasted more time.

A sudden smile broke across Tabby's face like
sunshine, and Acheron studied her intently, scan-
ning her delicate features, realising that there
could be an attractive female beneath the facade
of bolshie belligerence. He liked women femi-

nine, really, *really* feminine. She was crude and unkempt and the guardian of Olympia's granddaughter, he reminded himself doggedly, striving to concentrate on the most important element of the equation. And that was the child, *Amber*. He cursed the fact that he had not known of the connection sooner, cursed his own innate aversion to being tied down by anything other than business. He had no relatives, no loving relationships, no responsibility outside his company and that was how he liked his life. But not at the expense of basic decency. And his recollection of Olympia, who had frequently been kind and friendly to a boy everyone else had viewed as pure trouble, remained one of the few *good* memories Ash had of his childhood.

'Yes. I want to see the child as soon as possible,' Acheron confirmed.

Tabby tilted her head to one side, taken aback by his change of heart. 'What changed your mind?'

'I should have personally checked into her circumstances when I was informed of the guardianship,' Acheron breathed grimly, angry with himself for once at the elaborate and very protective support system around him that ensured that he was never troubled by too much detail about anything that might take his mind off business. 'But I will take care of that oversight now and be warned, Miss Glover, I will not support your application to adopt the little girl unless I reach the conclusion that you *are* a suitable carer. Thank you for your help, Stevos, but not for that last suggestion you made…' Sardonic dark eyes met the lawyer's frowning gaze. 'I'm afraid that idea belongs in fantasy land.'

CHAPTER TWO

'I COULD'VE DONE with some advance warning before you came to visit,' Tabby remarked thinly, after giving the uniformed chauffeur the address of the basement flat where she was currently staying, courtesy of her friend, Jack.

Jack, Sonia and Tabby had become fast friends and pseudo-siblings after passing their teenaged years in the same foster home.

Tabby eased slowly into the leather upholstered back seat of Acheron's unspeakably fancy limousine and studiously avoided staring starstruck at her surroundings but, dear heaven, it was a challenge not to stare at the built-in bar and entertainment centre. She had, however, enjoyed a mean moment of glorious one-upmanship when she sailed out of the front doors of the DT building with the doors held open by the same security guards who had, the hour before, manhandled her on the top floor.

'Obviously a warning would've been unwise. I need to see how you live without you putting on a special show for my benefit,' Acheron responded smoothly, flipping out a laptop onto the small table that emerged at the stab of a button from the division between front and back seats.

Tabby gritted her teeth at that frank admission. Any kind of fake special show was not an option open to her in the tiny bedsit that she was currently sharing with Amber. It was purely thanks to Jack, who was a small-time builder and property developer, that she still had Amber with her and had not already been forced to move into a hostel for the homeless and give up Sonia's daughter. It hurt that her long-term friendship with Sonia counted for nothing next to the remote blood tie Acheron Dimitrakos had shared with Troy. What had they been? Troy's gran had been a cousin of Acheron's mother, so Acheron was what…a third cousin or something in relation to Amber? Yet Tabby had known and loved Sonia since she was ten years old. They had met in the children's institution where they were both terrorised by the older kids. Tabby, having grown up in a violent home, had been much more used to defending herself than the younger girl. Sonia, after all, had once been a loved child in a decent family and tragically orphaned by the accident in which her parents died. In comparison, Tabby had been forcibly removed by the authorities from an abusive home and no longer knew whether her parents were alive or dead. There had been a few supervised visits with them after she was first taken away, many attempts to rehabilitate her mother and father and cobble the family back together, but in reality her parents proved to be more attached to their irresponsible lifestyle than they had ever been to their child.

Acheron Dimitrakos worked steadily at his laptop, making no effort to start up a conversation. Tabby compressed her generous mouth and studied him. She knew he had already decided that she was a rubbish person from the very bottom of the social pile. She knew he had taken one look and made judgements based on her appearance… and, doubtless, her use of bad language, she conceded with a sneaking feeling of shame.

But then she doubted he knew what it felt like

to be almost at the end of your tether. He was so…self-possessed, she decided resentfully, her violet gaze wandering over his bold bronzed profile, noting the slight curl in his thick black hair where it rested behind his ear and the extraordinary length of his dense inky-black eyelashes as he scrutinised the screen in front of him. Imagine a boyfriend with more impressive lashes than you have yourself, she ruminated, unimpressed, her soft mouth curling with disdain.

It annoyed her that he looked even more gorgeous in the flesh than he had in the magazine photographs. She had believed the photos must've been airbrushed to enhance his dark good looks but the evidence to the contrary was right before her. He had high aristocratic cheekbones, a perfectly straight nose and the wide, sensual mouth of a classic Greek statue. He was also extremely tall, broad-shouldered, narrow-hipped and long-legged—in fact, he was graced with every attractive male attribute possible.

Not a nice, caring person though, she reasoned staunchly, determined to concentrate on his flaws. Indeed, thinking of how he had outright refused to take any interest in Troy and Sonia's daughter, it was a challenge to understand why he should be suddenly bothering to come and see Amber now. She decided that she had made him feel guilty and that, after all, he *had* to have a conscience. Did that mean that he would support her application to adopt Amber? And even more importantly, would his opinion carry any weight with Social Services?

Acheron could not concentrate, which annoyed the hell out of him. Tabby Glover never sat still, and the constant movements of her slight small body on the seat beside him were an irritating distraction. He was too observant, he thought impatiently as he noted the bitten nails on her small hands, the shabbiness of her training shoes, the worn denim of jeans stretched taut over slender thighs, and he suppressed a sigh. He was out of his depth and although he had told Stevos to return to his office he was not enjoying the course he had set himself on. After all, what did he know about a young child's needs? Why did he feel guilty that he had already made up his mind to the hard fact that this young woman was not a fit sole guardian for a baby girl?

When the car came to a halt, Tabby slid out of the limo and bounced down the steps to stick her key in the front door of the basement flat. *Here goes,* she conceded nervously as she spread wide the door.

Ash froze one step inside, aghast at the indoor building site that comprised her accommodation. There was scaffolding, buckets and tools lying around, wires dangling everywhere, plasterboard walls. Tabby thrust open the first door to the left of the entrance.

Acheron followed her into a small room, packed with furniture and a table bearing a kettle and mini-oven and scattered with crumbs. Baby equipment littered almost every other surface. A teenage girl was seated on the bed with work files spread around her and when she saw Tabby she gathered up her files with a smile and stood up to leave. 'Amber's been great. She had a snack, enjoyed her bottle and she's been changed.'

'Thanks, Heather,' Tabby said quietly to the girl

who lived in the apartment above. 'I appreciate your help.'

The child was sitting up in the cot wedged between the bed and the wall on one side. Acheron surveyed the child from a safe distance, noting the mop of black curls, the big brown eyes and the instant dazzling smile that rewarded Tabby's appearance.

'How's my darling girl?' Tabby asked, leaning over the cot to scoop up the little girl and hug her tight. Chubby arms wrapped round her throat while curious brown eyes inspected Acheron over Tabby's shoulder.

'What age is she?' Ash enquired.

'You should know,' Tabby said drily. 'She's over six months old.'

'Do the authorities know you're keeping her here?'

A flush of uneasy colour warmed Tabby's cheeks as she sat down on the bed because Amber was getting heavier by the day. 'No. I gave them Jack's address. He's a friend and he bought this apartment to renovate and sell on. He's allowing us to stay here out of the goodness of his heart. He hasn't the space for us at his own place.'

'How can you live in such a squalid dwelling with a young child and believe that you're doing the best you can for her?' Acheron condemned.

'Well, for a start, it's not squalid!' Tabby flared defensively and hurriedly rose to set Amber back into her cot. 'It's clean. We have heating and light and there's a fully functional bathroom through that door.' She pointed a hand to the opposite wall, and the gesture fell down in effectiveness because her arm shook and she hurriedly lowered it again. Tears were suddenly stinging the back of her eyes, and her head was starting to thump with the onset of a stress headache. 'For the moment I'm just doing the best I can but we're *managing*.'

'But you're not managing well enough,' Ash stated curtly. 'You shouldn't be keeping a young child in accommodation like this.'

Her brow pulsing with the band of tension tightening round it, Tabby lifted her hands to release the weight of her hair from the ponytail. Acheron watched a torrent of long blonde hair fall down to her waist and finally saw something he liked about her appearance: blonde hair that was natural unless he was very much mistaken, for that pale mass had no dark roots or streaky highlights.

'I'm doing the very best I can,' Tabby countered firmly, wondering why he was staring at her, her self-conscious streak on override, her pride still hurting from the 'squalid' comment.

'And how are you supporting yourself?' Acheron asked with a curled lip.

'I'm still cleaning. I didn't lose all my clients when I had to close my business down, and those I kept I'm still working for. I take Amber with me to the jobs. Most of my clients are out at work anyway so her coming with me doesn't bother them,' she admitted grudgingly. 'Take a look at her. She's clean and well fed and happy. We're rarely apart.'

Ash assimilated the information with a grim twist of his expressive mouth. 'I'm sorry, but your best isn't good enough. Nothing I've seen here will convince me otherwise. You don't have a proper home for the child. You're clearly living on the poverty line—'

'Money isn't everything!' Tabby protested. 'I love her and she loves me.'

Ash watched the slender blonde lean over the cot rail to gently stroke the little girl's head and saw the answering sunny smile that the gesture evoked. No such love or tenderness had featured in his childhood experience, and he fully recognised the fact, but he was also bone-deep practical and not given to changing his mind mid-course. 'Love isn't enough on its own. If you had a supportive family to back you and a proper home to raise her in I might feel differently, but you on your own with her in this dismal room and dragging her out with you to cleaning jobs is *wrong*,' he pronounced with strong conviction. 'She could do better than this, she *should* have better than this and it is *her* needs and not your own that you should be weighing in the balance.'

'Are you saying that I'm selfish?' Tabby prompted in disbelief, because she had given up so much that was important to her to take care first of Sonia, after she had suffered her first stroke, and ultimately her baby daughter.

Beneath the shocked onslaught of eyes the colour of rain-washed amethysts, Acheron's stubborn jaw line clenched hard and his mouth compressed. 'Yes. You have obviously done the best you can and given her continuity of care since her mother's death but now it's time for you to step back and put her best interests ahead of your own personal feelings.'

The tears glistening in Tabby's eyes overflowed, marking silvery trails on her cheeks, and for the first time in years Acheron felt like a real bastard and yet he had only told the truth as he saw it. *I love her and she loves me.* Yes, he could see the strength of the bond before him but it couldn't cover up the cracks in the long-term struggle for survival he saw for them both. Olympia's grandchild deserved more. Yet how did he put a price on the love and then dismiss it as if it were worthless?

'What age are you?' he pressed.

'Twenty-five.'

'I should've dealt with this situation when it first came up,' Acheron acknowledged grimly, thinking that she was surely far too young and immature to take on such a burden and that he should have taken immediate action to resolve the situation the instant the guardianship issue arose. It was his fault that Tabby Glover had been left to struggle on with the child while becoming more and more dangerously attached to her charge.

'Not if it meant parting Amber and me sooner,' Tabby argued. 'Can't you understand how much I care about her? Her mother and I became best friends when we were kids, and I'll be able to share my memories of her parents with her when she's old enough to want that information. Surely there's something you could do to help?'

But on a personal level, Acheron didn't want to be involved. He always avoided emotional situations and responsibilities that fell outside company business, and it had been that very detachment that had first roused his late father's concern that his only son should have set himself on such a solitary path.

Tabby searched Acheron's handsome features, marvelling at his masculine perfection even as she appraised the glitter of his dark-as-jet eyes and the hard tension round his wide, sensual mouth. 'I'll do anything it takes to keep her...'

Acheron frowned, his brow furrowing. 'What's that supposed to mean?'

'What do you think? I'm desperate to keep Amber. If you have any suggestions on how I can be a better parent to her, I'm willing to listen and take advice,' Tabby extended with the new-found humility of fear.

'I thought you were offering me sex,' Acheron confided bluntly.

'Seriously?' Tabby gasped in shock at that misconception. 'Does that happen to you a lot? I mean…women… just offering?'

Acheron nodded cool confirmation.

Her violet eyes widened in astonishment and she lifted her head, pale blonde hair cascading in a silken tangle round her shoulders with the movement. In the space of a split second she travelled from *possibly* pretty to decidedly beautiful in Acheron's estimation, and desire kindled; a desire he neither wanted nor intended to act on. His body was stubborn, though, and the pulse of heaviness at his groin was utterly disobedient to his brain, throwing up outrageous images of her lying on his bed, that lovely swathe of hair spread over his chest, that lush mouth gainfully employed in pleasuring him. He gritted his perfect white teeth, suppressing the outrageous fantasy, furiously conscious of the child's innocent presence and his unprecedented loss of self-discipline.

'Women just offer themselves? No wonder you're so full of yourself,' Tabby remarked helplessly, aware of the tension in the atmosphere, but unsure of its source as she stared back at him. She liked looking at him, didn't know why or exactly what it was about those lean sculpted features that fascinated her so much. But as she collided with his stunning dark-as-midnight gaze, liquid warmth surged between her legs and her nipples tightened, a message even she couldn't ignore or deny. He attracted her. The filthy rich Greek with his dazzling good looks and hard-as-granite heart *attracted* her. How foolish and deceptive physical chemistry could be, she reflected ruefully, embarrassment colouring her pale cheeks.

I'll do anything it takes to keep her... And suddenly Acheron, rigid with the force of his self-control, was reasoning with a new and unfamiliar sense of freedom to think outside the box and he was thinking, Why not? Why the hell not? Possibly Stevos's bright idea had not been as off the wall as it had first seemed. He and this strange girl both wanted something from each other, and he could certainly ensure that Amber benefitted from the deal in every way, thereby satisfying his uneasy conscience where the child was concerned.

'There *is* a way you could keep Amber with you.' Ash dangled the bait straight away, as always impatient to plunge to the heart of the matter.

Tabby leant forward where she sat, wide violet eyes intent on him. *'How?'*

'We could apply as a couple to adopt her—'

Thoroughly disconcerted by that unexpected suggestion, Tabby blinked. 'As a couple?'

'With my backing it could be achieved but we would need to be married first,' Ash delivered smoothly, deciding there and then that he would not admit the truth that he would have a great deal riding on the arrangement as well. That acknowledgement would tip the power balance between them and he refused to take that unnecessary risk and find himself being blackmailed. The less she knew, the less power she would have.

Astonishment was stamped on her small oval face. *'Married?'*

'For the sake of the adoption application. I should think that the most traditional approach would have the likeliest and quickest chance of success.'

'Let me get this straight...you're saying you would be willing to marry me to help me get permission to adopt Amber?' Tabby breathed in frank disbelief.

Acheron dealt her a sardonic look. 'Naturally I'm not suggesting a proper marriage. I'm suggesting the legal ceremony and a joint application to adopt her. We would then only have to give the appearance that we are living below the same roof for as long as it takes to complete the proceedings.'

So, not a real marriage, a *fake* one, she mused, but even so she was still transfixed by the concept and the idea that he might be willing to go to such lengths to help her. 'But why would you do that for us? A couple of months ago, you simply dismissed the idea that you could have any obligation towards Amber.'

'I wasn't aware then that she was Olympia Carolis's grandchild—'

'Olympia…who?' Tabby queried blankly.

'Troy's mother. I only knew her by the name she had before she married. I knew her when I was a child because she worked for my mother and lived with us,' Acheron volunteered with pronounced reluctance. 'I lost all contact with that side of the family after my mother died. But I liked Olympia. She was a good woman.'

'Yet you don't have the slightest true interest in Amber,' Tabby commented with a frown of incomprehension. 'You haven't even tried to hold her.'

'I'm not accustomed to babies and I don't want to frighten her,' Acheron excused himself glibly and watched her process his polite lie. 'I should've taken a greater interest in the child when I was first informed that I was one of her guardians. Your situation would not have reached crisis point had I accepted that commitment and taken my share of the responsibility.'

His admission of fault soothed Tabby, who had not been prepared for that amount of candour from him. He had made a mistake and was man enough to acknowledge it, an attitude that she respected. He had also moved a step closer to the cot and Amber, always a friendly baby, was beaming up at him in clear expectation of being lifted. But his lean brown hands clenched into taut stillness by his side, and she recognised that if anyone was frightened it was not Amber, it was *him*. Of course, he was an only child, and she assumed he had had little contact with young children because his rigid inhibited stance close to the baby spoke loudly for him.

'So, you've changed your mind and you think I should adopt her?'

'Not quite that,' Ash declared levelly. 'If we go ahead with this, I will be on the spot to oversee Amber's welfare and if I'm satisfied that you're a capable mother, I will release her fully into your care after we divorce. Naturally I will also ensure that when we part you have a proper home to raise her in.'

In other words, she would be on probation as a parent for the duration of the fake marriage, which was not good news on her terms. But Acheron Dimitrakos had to *really* care about what happened to Amber to be willing to get so involved and make such a sacrifice as marrying a stranger for the child's benefit alone, she thought ruefully, suddenly ashamed of her prejudices about him.

He would be killing two birds with one stone, Ash decided with satisfaction, solving all his problems in one decisive act. He would choose a discreet location for the ceremony but at the same time, if anyone was to be expected to believe that they were a couple and the marriage genuine, she would have to undergo a major makeover first.

'I'll take you home with me now,' Acheron pronounced. 'Bring the baby…leave everything else. My staff will pack your possessions.'

'Are you joking? Walk out the door with a strange man and move in with him?' Tabby breathed in stark disbelief. 'Do I look that naive and trusting?'

Acheron studied her levelly. 'You only get one chance with me and, I warn you, I'm not a patient man. I can't leave you and the child living here like this and, if we decide to go ahead with the marriage and adoption plan, there are things to be done, forms to be filled in without further waste of time.'

Tabby leapt up. As he shifted his feet in their highly polished leather shoes and elevated a sleek black brow in expectation he emanated impatience in invisible sparks, filling the atmosphere with tension. He thought he was doing her a favour and that she ought to jump to attention and follow his instructions and, because that was true, she wasn't going to argue with him. In fact, just for once, she was going to keep her ready tongue glued to the roof of her mouth and play nice to keep him happy and willing to help. Yes, she would trust him, but common sense suggested that a male as rich and gorgeous as he was had many more tempting sexual outlets than a woman as ordinary as she was.

'OK...' Tabby stuffed nappies and bottles and a tub of formula milk into the worn baby bag, and threaded Amber's chubby arms into a jacket that was slightly too small before strapping her into the car seat that she had had no use for since she had had to sell her car.

Acheron was already on his phone to his PA, telling her to engage an emergency nanny because he had no plans to trail the baby out shopping with them. The deal was done, only the details had to be dealt with now and he was in his element.

Ash stayed on the phone for the first ten minutes of their journey, rapping out instructions, making arrangements, telling Stevos to make a start on the paperwork. For the first time in a week he felt he was back in control of his life and it felt good. He stole a reluctant glance at Tabby, engaged in keeping Amber occupied by pointing out things through the windows. The awareness that Tabby Glover was going to prove very useful to him compressed his hard mouth because he was convinced that she would be difficult.

'Where are you taking us?' she asked, still in something of a daze after that discussion about adoption and marriage. She was scarcely able to credit that her and Amber's luck had turned a magical corner because Acheron Dimitrakos bore not the slightest resemblance to a fairy godmother.

'Back to my apartment where we will drop off…Amber,' Acheron advanced warily.

'And who are you planning to drop her off with? Your staff? *That's* not going to happen,' Tabby began forcefully.

'I have organised a nanny, who will be waiting for us. We will then go shopping to buy you some clothes.'

'Amber doesn't need a nanny and I don't need clothes.'

Acheron treated her to a scornful dark appraisal that burned colour into her cheeks. 'You're hardly dressed suitably. If we're to put on a convincing act, you need clothes,' he contradicted.

Anger flared in her violet eyes and her head turned sharply. 'I *don't* need—'

'Just say the word and I'll return you both to your clean and comfy basement,' Acheron told her in a lethally quiet tone of warning.

Tabby sucked in a sudden deep breath and held

it, recognising that she was trapped, something she never ever allowed herself to be because being trapped meant being vulnerable. But if she said no, refused to toe the line, she would lose Amber for good. There would be no coming back from that development because once Amber was removed from her care, she would be gone for all time.

Had Acheron Dimitrakos been right to censure her selfishness in wanting to keep Sonia's daughter as her own? It was a painful thought. She hated to think that he could know better about anything but she knew that outsiders often saw more clearly than those directly involved. All she had to offer Amber was love, and he had said love wasn't enough. But Tabby valued love much more highly because she hadn't received it as a child and had often longed for the warm sense of acceptance, well-being and security that a loving parent could bestow. Only time would tell if Amber herself would agree that Tabby had made the wisest decision on her behalf.

Amber hugged Tabby in the lift on the way up to Acheron's apartment, the little girl clinging in reaction to Tabby's increasing tension. Acheron stood poised in the far corner of the mirrored compartment, a comfortable six feet three inches of solid masculine detachment. Tabby studied him in growing frustration, noting the aloof quality in his gaze, the forbidding cool of his lean, strong face. He was so unemotional about everything that he infuriated her. Here she was awash with conflicting emotions, terrified she was doing the wrong thing, putting her feelings rather than Amber's needs first…and whose fault was that? She had not doubted her ability to be a good mother until Acheron Dimitrakos crossed her path. Now she was facing the challenge of also surrendering her pride and her independence to meet his expectations.

'I don't think this is going to work,' she told him helplessly. 'We mix like oil and water.'

'A meeting of true minds is not required,' Ash imparted with sardonic bite. 'Stop arguing about every little thing. That irritates me.'

'A nanny is not a little thing. Who is she?'

'A highly trained professional from a reputable source. I would not put the child at risk.'

His intense dark eyes challenged her, and she looked away, her cheeks burning, her mouth dry, her grip on Amber still a little tighter than it needed to be. For a split second she felt as though Amber were the only sure element left in the world that he was tearing apart and threatening to rebuild. He intimidated her, a truth that made her squirm. Yet he was willing to help her keep Amber, she reminded herself doggedly, and that should be her bottom line. Whatever it took she should bite the bullet and focus on the end game, not how bad it might feel getting there.

'Won't the sort of marriage you suggested be illegal?' she heard herself ask him abruptly. 'You know, a marriage that's just a fake?'

'Why would it be illegal?' he countered with icy cool. 'What goes on within any marriage is private.'

'But our marriage would be an act of deception.'

'You're splitting hairs. No one would be harmed by the deception. The marriage would simply present us as a conventional couple keen to adopt.'

'You're hopelessly out of date. Lots of couples don't get married these days,' Tabby pointed out.

'In my family we always get married when it comes to child-rearing,' Acheron told her smoothly.

That's right, remind me that I'm not from the same world! Tabby thought furiously, a flush of antagonism warming her face as embarrassment threatened to swallow her alive. Her parents had not been married and had probably never even thought of getting married to regularise her birth.

Her gaze strayed inexorably back to him until she connected with smoky dark deep-set eyes that made her tummy lurch and leap and heat rise in her pelvis. There was just something about him, she thought furiously, dragging her attention from him as the lift doors whirred open and she hastily stepped out into a hallway, something shockingly sexy and dangerous that broke through her defences. She did not understand how he could act like an unfeeling block of superior ice and still have that effect on her.

CHAPTER THREE

THE NANNY, COMPLETE with a uniform that suggested she belonged to the very highest echelon of qualified nannies, awaited Acheron and Tabby in the spacious hall of Acheron's apartment and within minutes she had charmed Amber out of Tabby's arms and borne her off.

'Let's go,' Acheron urged impatiently. 'We have a lot to accomplish.'

'I don't like shopping,' Tabby breathed, literally cringing at the prospect of him paying for her clothes.

'Neither do I. In fact, usually the closest I get to shopping with a woman is giving her a credit card,' Acheron confided silkily. 'But I don't trust you to buy the right stuff.'

Mutinously silent as she slid back into the waiting limousine in the underground car park, Tabby shrugged a slight shoulder, determined not to battle with him when it was a battle she could not win. Even so, he could dress her up all he liked but it wouldn't change the person she truly was. No, she would be sensible and look on the clothing as a necessary prop for their masquerade, another move in what already felt more like a game than reality because in no realistic dimension did a girl like her marry a guy as rich and good-looking as him.

A personal shopper awaited them at Harrods where, surprisingly enough, Acheron appeared to be in his element. Tabby did not attempt to impose her opinions and she hovered while Acheron pointed out what he liked and the correct size was lifted from the rail. She soon found herself in a changing cubicle with a heap of garments.

'Come out,' Ash instructed impatiently. 'I want to see you in the pink dress.'

Suppressing a groan, Tabby snaked into the classy little cocktail frock, reached down to flip off her socks and walked barefoot out of the cubicle.

Acheron frowned as she came to a halt and he strolled round her, staring at her slight figure in surprise. 'I didn't realise you were so tiny.'

Tabby gnawed at her lower lip, knowing she had skipped too many meals in recent months, painfully aware that she was too thin and that what delicate curves she had possessed had shrunk along with any excess body fat. 'I'm a lot stronger than I look,' she said defensively.

Acheron studied her doll-like dimensions with unabashed interest, his narrowed gaze running from her fragile shoulders down to her pale slender legs. He could've easily lifted her with one hand. He liked curves on a woman yet there was an aesthetically pleasing aspect to the pure delicacy of her build. Her breasts barely made an indent in the bodice of the dress and her hips made no imprint at all. Yet with that tousled mane of long blonde hair highlighting her pale oval face and bright violet eyes, she looked unusual and extraordinarily appealing. He wondered if he would crush her in bed and then squashed that crazy thought dead because sex would naturally not be featuring in their agreement. As she turned away, he froze, taken aback by the sight of the colourful rose tattoo marring the pale skin of her left forearm.

'That dress won't do,' Acheron told the assistant thinly. 'She needs a dress with sleeves to cover that.'

Gooseflesh crept over Tabby's exposed skin, and she clamped a hand over the skin marking she had forgotten about. Beneath her fingers she could feel the rougher skin of the scar tissue that the tattoo pretty much concealed from view, and her heart dropped to the pit of her stomach, remembered feelings of bitter pain and heartache gripping her in spite of the years that had passed since the wound was first inflicted. She had made the clear considered choice that she could live better with the tattoo than she could with that constant reminder of her wretched childhood catching her unawares every time she looked in the mirror. Of course, the skin ink wasn't perfect because the skin surface beneath it was far from perfect and the tattooist had warned her of the fact in advance. As it was, the rose, albeit a little blurred in its lines, had done the job it was designed to do, hiding the scar and providing a burial place for the bad memories. Only very rarely did Tabby think about it.

'How could you disfigure your body with that?' Acheron demanded in a driven undertone, his revulsion unhidden.

'It's of a good luck charm. I've had it for years,' Tabby told him unsteadily, her face pale and set.

The personal shopper was already approaching with a long-sleeved dress, and Tabby returned to the cubicle, her skin clammy now with the aftermath of shock—the shock of being forced back, however briefly, into her violent past. The rose was her lucky charm, which concealed the vivid reminder of what could happen when you loved someone unworthy of that trust. So, he didn't like tattoos; well, what was that to her? She put on the new dress, smoothed down the sleeves and, mustering her self-possession, she emerged again.

Acheron stared her up and down, his beautiful face curiously intent. Heat blossomed in her cheeks as he studied her with smouldering dark eyes, his tension palpable. Desire flickered low in her pelvis like kindling yearning for a spark, and she felt that craving shoot through every fibre of her body, from the dryness of her mouth to the swelling sensitivity of her nipples and the honeyed heat between her thighs. It made her feel light-headed and oddly intoxicated, and she blinked rapidly, severely disconcerted by the feelings.

'That will do,' he pronounced thickly.

She wanted to touch him so badly she had to clench her hands into fists to prevent herself from reaching out and making actual contact. She felt like a wasp being drawn to a honey trap and fiercely fought her reactions with every scrap of self-control left to her. Don't touch, *don't touch*, a little voice warned in the back of her head, but evidently he was listening to a different voice as he stalked closer and reached for her hands, pulling them into his, urging her closer, forcing her fingers to loosen within his grasp.

And Tabby looked up at him and froze, literally not daring to breathe. That close his eyes were no longer dark but a downright amazing and glorious swirl of honey, gold and caramel tones, enhanced by the spiky black lashes she envied. His fingers were feathering over hers with a gentleness she had not expected from so big and powerful a man and little tremors of response were filtering through her, undermining her self-control. She knew she wanted those expert hands on her body exploring much more secret places, and colour rose in her cheeks because she also knew she was out of her depth and drowning. In an abrupt movement, she wrenched her hands free and turned away, momentarily shutting her eyes in a gesture of angry self-loathing.

'Try on the rest of the clothes,' Acheron instructed coolly, not a flicker of lingering awareness in his dark deep voice.

Hot-faced, Tabby vanished back into the cubicle. Evidently he pressed all her buttons, and she had to stop letting him do that to her, had to stand firm. Of course he was sexy: he was a womaniser. He had insulted her with that crack about her tattoo and had then somehow switched that moment into something else by catching her hands in his and just looking at her. But she wasn't some impressionable little airhead vulnerable to the merest hint of interest from an attractive man, was she? Well, she *was* a virgin, she acknowledged grudgingly, as always stifling her unease about that glaring lack in her experience with men. After all she had not intentionally chosen to retain her virginity; it had just happened that way. No man had ever succeeded in making her want to get that close to him, and she had no plans to share a bed with someone simply to find out what it was like.

And then Acheron Dimitrakos had come along and turned everything she thought she knew on its head. For, although he attracted her, she didn't like him and didn't trust him either, so what did that say about her? That she had a reckless streak just like her long-lost and unlamented parents?

Tension seethed through Acheron. What the hell was the matter with him? He had been on the edge of crushing that soft, luscious mouth beneath his, close to wrecking the non-sexual relationship he envisaged between them. Impersonal would work the best and it shouldn't be that difficult, he reasoned impatiently, for they had nothing in common.

He watched her emerge again, clad in cropped wool trousers, high heels and a slinky little burgundy cashmere cardigan. She looked really good. She cleaned up incredibly well, he acknowledged grudgingly, gritting his teeth together as his gaze instinctively dropped to the sweet pouting swell of her small breasts beneath the clingy top.

He had done what he had to do, he reminded himself grimly. She was perfect for his purposes, for she had as much riding on the success of their arrangement as he had. Thankfully nothing in his life was going to change in the slightest: he had found the perfect wife, a non-wife...

He left Tabby alone with the shopper in the lingerie department and she chose the basics before heading for the children's department and choosing an entire new wardrobe for Amber, her heart singing at the prospect of seeing the little girl in new clothes that fitted her properly. The chauffeur saw to the stowing of her many bags in the capacious boot of the limousine, and she climbed in beside Acheron, who was talking on the phone in French. She recognised the language from lessons at school and raised her brows. So, that was at least *three* languages he spoke: Greek, English and now French. She refused to be impressed.

'We'll dine out tonight,' Acheron pronounced, putting the phone away.

'Why the heck would you want to do that?' Tabby demanded in dismay at the prospect.

'If we want to give the appearance of a normal couple, we need to be seen out together. Wear that dress.'

'Oh…' Tabby said nothing more while she wondered what social horrors dining out with him would entail. She had never eaten out in a fancy restaurant, having always cravenly avoided such formal occasions, intimidated by the prospect of too much cutlery and superior serving staff, who would surely quickly spot that she was a take-away girl at heart.

Two hours later, having showered and changed, Acheron opened the safe in his bedroom wall to remove a ring case he hadn't touched in years. The fabled emerald, which had reputedly once adorned a maharajah's crown, had belonged to his late mother and would do duty as an engagement ring. The very thought of putting the priceless jewel on Tabby's finger chilled Acheron's anti-commitment gene to the marrow, and he squared his broad shoulders, grateful that the engagement and the marriage that would follow would be one hundred per cent fake.

'Fine feathers make fine birds' had been one of her last foster mother's favourite sayings, Tabby recalled as she put on mascara, guiltily enjoying the fact that she had both the peace and the time to use cosmetics again. Make-up had been one of the first personal habits to fall by the wayside once she took on full-time care of Amber. But the nanny had been hired to work until eleven that night, leaving Amber free to dress up and go out like a lady of leisure. A *lady*? She grimaced at the word, doubting she could ever match that lofty description, and ran a brush through her freshly washed hair before grabbing the clutch that matched the shoes and leaving the room.

Acheron's apartment was vast, much bigger than she had expected. Tabby and Amber had been relegated to rooms at the very foot of the bedroom corridor, well away from the main reception areas as well as the principal bedroom suite, which seemed to be sited up a spiral staircase off the main hall. Acheron Dimitrakos lived like a king, she conceded with a shake of her head, wide-eyed at the opulence of the furnishings surrounding her and the fresh flowers blooming on every surface. They truly did come from different worlds. But the one trait they shared, she sensed, was an appreciation of hard slog and its rewards, so she hoped he would understand why she needed to continue to work.

'Put it on,' Acheron advised in the hall, planting an emerald ring unceremoniously into the palm of her hand.

Tabby frowned down at the gleaming jewel. 'What's it for?'

'Engagement ring…marriage?' Acheron groaned. 'Sometimes you're very slow on the uptake.'

Tabby rammed the beautiful ring down over her knuckle and squinted down at it, her colour high. 'I didn't know we were going for frills. I assumed you would choose more of a basic-package approach.'

'Since we'll be getting married pretty quickly and without a big splash our charade needs to look more convincing from the outset.'

'I'm already living with you and wearing clothes you bought for me,' she parried flatly. 'Isn't that enough of a show?'

'Many couples live together without marrying, many women have worn clothing I paid for,' Acheron derided. 'What we have has to look more serious.'

The restaurant was dimly lit and intimate and their table probably the best in the room. Certainly the attention that came their way from the staff was so constant that Tabby found it almost claustrophobic. Having studiously ignored her during the drive while talking on his phone, Acheron finally allowed himself the indulgence of looking at his bride-to-be. Her blonde mane tumbled round her shoulders framing a vivid and delicate little face dominated by violet eyes and a lush fuchsia-tinted mouth. He couldn't take his eyes off that mouth, a mouth modelled to make a man think of sin and sinning.

'How am I performing so far as your dress-up doll?' Tabby enquired mockingly to take her mind off the fact that she had still not established which knife and fork to use with the salad being brought to them.

'You answer back too much but you look amazing in the right clothes,' Acheron conceded, startling her with that compliment. 'So far I'm very satisfied with our bargain, and you can be assured that I will play my part.'

As he reached for one fork she reached for another and then changed course mid-movement, her gaze welded to his lean brown hands. *Just copy him*, her brain urged her.

'I've applied for a special licence. The legalities should be in place in time for the ceremony to be held on Thursday,' Acheron delivered. 'My lawyer is making all the arrangements and has contacted Social Services on our behalf with regard to our plans for Amber.'

'My word, he's a fast mover,' Tabby remarked breathlessly.

'You told me you didn't want the child to go into foster care,' he reminded her.

Her skin turned clammy at that daunting reminder of the unknown destination that would have awaited Amber had Tabby not gained his support. 'I don't but there are things we still haven't discussed. What am I supposed to do while we're pretending to be married?'

A winged ebony brow lifted. '*Do*? Nothing. You concentrate on being a mother and occasionally a wife. I will expect you to make a couple of appearances with me at public events. That is the sole commitment you have to make to me.'

'That's great because I want to start up my business again…in a small way,' Tabby admitted abruptly.

His handsome features clenched hard. 'No. That's out of the question. The child deserves a full-time mother.'

Tabby couldn't believe her ears. 'Most mothers work—'

'I will cover your financial requirements,' Acheron delivered with unquenchable cool. 'For the foreseeable future you will put the child's needs first and you will not work.'

Tabby gritted her teeth. 'I don't want to take your money.'

'Tough,' Acheron slotted in succinctly.

'You can't tell me what I can and can't do.'

'Can't I?'

Tabby's pulse had quickened until it felt as if it were beating in the foot of her throat, obstructing her ability to breathe and speak. Frustrated rage lay behind her choked silence as she stared across the table at him, her small face taut and pale. He was pulling strings as if she were a puppet. And wasn't she exactly that?

A chill settled over her rage, safely enclosing it. He was willing to help her to adopt Amber and she was stuck with his outdated idealistic attitude whether she liked it or not. Yes, she could walk away from him but if she did so she would also be walking away from the child she loved. And that, Tabby reflected hollowly, she could not do.

Amber had tugged at Tabby's heartstrings from the day she was born and Sonia was too weak, having suffered her first stroke within hours of the birth, even to hold her daughter. Consequently, for as long as Tabby needed Acheron's support she would have to conform to *his* expectations. Facing and accepting that ugly frightening truth had to be one of the most humbling experiences Tabby had ever known because it ran contrary to every tenet she had lived by since adulthood. The threat of no longer being in full charge of her life genuinely terrified Tabby.

'You seem to have lost your appetite,' Ash remarked, watching her move the food around her plate without lifting anything to her ripe pink mouth.

It was a steak cooked rare, not the way she liked it. But then she had coped with the menu being written in pretentious French simply by making the exact same menu choices as he had.

'You killed my appetite,' Tabby countered thinly.

A forbidding look flitted across his chiselled features. 'If restarting your business means that much to you, you should give up your desire to adopt a child, who will need much more of your time than you could give her as an independent businesswoman.'

Well, that certainly put his point of view across, Tabby conceded ruefully, sipping her water, ignoring the full wineglass beside it. She never touched alcohol, didn't trust the effect it might have on her, feared it might even awaken a craving she might find hard to control. She couldn't argue with Acheron Dimitrakos because setting up her business again *would* demand a great deal of her time. She compressed her lips, reasonably certain she could've coped without short-changing Amber but questioning for the first time whether or not that would have been fair to the child she loved. After all, she had personally never enjoyed the luxury of being a full-time mother and perhaps it would be more sensible to give that lifestyle a shot rather than dismissing it out of hand.

'Are we on the same page?' Acheron Dimitrakos asked impatiently over the cheese and crackers.

Mouth full at last of something she wanted to eat, Tabby nodded while trying not to imagine what it would feel like to be financially dependent on a man for the first time in her life.

As they emerged from the restaurant, Acheron banded an arm round her stiff spine, and she blinked in bewilderment at the daunting acknowledgement that they were literally surrounded by photographers. 'Smile,' he instructed her flatly.

And, hating it, she did as she was told.

'What was that all about?' she demanded once they were driving away.

'Public proof of our relationship,' Acheron supplied drily. 'There'll be an announcement of our engagement in *The Times* tomorrow.'

What relationship? Tabby thought with wry amusement. He said jump, she said how high? That was not a relationship, it was a dictatorship, but possibly he didn't know the difference.

The plaintive cry roused Acheron from a sound sleep. He listened for a while but the noise continued. After a moment, he rolled out of bed with a curse on his lips and reached the bedroom door, before groaning out loud and stalking back to rummage through a drawer and extract a pair of jeans. He hated having guests. He hated any interruption to his usual routine. But Tabby was a better option than a real wife, he reminded himself with satisfaction, and a good deal less likely to develop ambitious ideas about hanging on to her privileged position.

He pushed open the door of the nursery and saw the baby in the cot. It was kicking its arms and legs in furious activity, its little face screwed up as it loosed a wail that would have wakened the dead. Only, apparently, not her wannabe adoptive mother. Ash hovered by the cot, his wide, sensual mouth on a downward curve. The baby sat up in a flash and looked expectant, even lifted its arms as if she expected him to haul her to freedom. It looked far too lively for a baby supposed to be sleeping.

'No more crying,' Ash decreed firmly. 'I don't like crying.'

The baby's arms lowered, its rosebud mouth jutting out in a pout while its bright brown eyes studied him uncertainly.

'You see, crying gets you nowhere,' Ash explained helpfully.

Another heartbroken sob emanated from the baby. She looked incredibly sad and lonely, and Ash stifled a groan.

'Aren't you going to lift her? She needs comforting,' Tabby murmured from the doorway, studying the little tableau of inflexible male and needy baby. It was infuriating to register that she couldn't take her eyes off him when he was wearing only a pair of jeans. He had a six-pack that could have rivalled a top athlete's and his lean, muscular bronzed chest was state-of-the-art perfection, showcasing a male body that could have played a starring role in any female fantasy.

'Why would I lift her?' Ash enquired with a raised brow, flashing her a glance and noticing in that one brief look that she was wearing a pale nightdress that revealed more than it concealed of her tiny body while she stood with her back turned to the light in the corridor. He glimpsed delicate little pink nipples and a pale shadowy vee between her thighs, and his body reacted with instantaneous arousal.

'Because if you expect our adoption application to impress the powers-that-be, you need to be confident that you can handle Amber.'

'I will be perfectly confident if the situation demands that of me, but at this hour of the day it would be very unwise to remove her from the cot,' he declared. 'She's there for the whole night. It's two in the morning, in case you haven't noticed. Why raise her hopes by lifting her?'

Amber released another howl and, gripped by

frustration, Tabby marched over to the cot, swept up the little girl and settled her without ceremony into Ash's arms. 'If she has a nightmare she needs comforting. She needs to know someone is there for her and a little cuddle usually soothes her.'

Amber was as shocked as Acheron to find herself in his arms. Wide brown eyes anxiously observed him. 'Cuddle?' Ash almost whispered the word in appalled disbelief. 'You actually expect me to cuddle her?'

CHAPTER FOUR

WITH A GASP of irritation, Tabby removed Amber from his awkward hold and pressed her close. 'Skin-to-skin contact is important,' she demonstrated, kissing Amber's hot brow.

'I'm not doing the kissing stuff either,' Acheron breathed witheringly.

'Then smooth her hair, rub her back, make her feel secure in other ways,' Tabby advised ruefully. 'Stop being so resistant to my suggestions.'

'And how do you suggest I do that? With a personality transplant?' Acheron derided. 'I'm no good with kids. I have no experience of that sort of affection.'

'It's never too late to learn,' Tabby told him with determination, settling Amber carefully back into his arms. 'Hold her closer, pet her. And please don't tell me you have no experience of petting women.'

'I don't pet them. I have sex with them. This is

not an appropriate conversation to have around a child!' Acheron bit out in exasperation.

Picking up on his annoyance, Amber whimpered. He spread his fingers across her back in an uneasy rubbing motion.

'Bring her closer,' Tabby urged, approaching him to tuck the baby into the curve of his shoulder. 'She's not going to bite.'

Acheron could never recall feeling quite so tense or uncomfortable. He knew what she wanted from him but he didn't want to do it. Then he thought of DT Industries, which would be one hundred per cent his only after the wedding, and he held the baby against him, deeming it a sacrifice worthy of such a result.

'And talk to her,' Tabby suggested.

'What about?' Acheron demanded with perfect seriousness, freezing as the baby nestled close of its own volition, disconcerted by the alien warmth and weight of her as she dug little hands into the flesh of his shoulder.

'Stocks and shares if you like. It doesn't matter at this age. It's the sound and tone of your voice that matters,' Tabby explained.

Acheron mumbled a Greek nursery rhyme.

'And if you walk around the room with her, it might make you feel more relaxed.'

Acheron gritted his teeth and started to tell the baby exactly what he thought of Tabby in Greek, careful to keep the antagonism out of his voice. Amber looked up at him with big trusting brown eyes, and he marvelled at her ability to award that amount of trust to a complete stranger. If the baby could try, he could as well even if it did stick in his throat to be listening to Tabby's instructions and following them. She maddened him, he acknowledged grimly, gently rubbing Amber's back as he talked. The baby slowly rested its head down on his shoulder.

'Give her to me,' Tabby murmured. 'She's going back to sleep.'

'And so ends lesson one,' Acheron mocked as she settled Amber back into the cot and covered her again. Only it was not the child he was watching but Tabby. The pale grey silk glimmered in the dull light from the corridor, splaying across her thighs, outlining the plump little curves of her derriere as she bent over the cot rail, prominent nipples visible against the flimsy fabric as she straightened again.

Acheron was hard as a rock by the time he completed that far from fleeting appraisal. 'You might want to cover up more around me,' he commented. 'Or is this a come-on?'

Her violet eyes flew wide as she faltered at the doorway, and she flashed him an incredulous glance back over a narrow shoulder. 'Do you think you're irresistible or something?'

Acheron strode over to the doorway. 'You can't be that innocent. Men are fairly predictable when there is so much bare skin on display.'

'I am not on display,' Tabby countered furiously, crossing her arms defensively over her lightly clad length, sharply disconcerted by the idea that he could see her body beneath the nightie. 'When I came in I had no idea you would be in here.'

Acheron closed a hand around her wrist and tugged her into the corridor, shutting the door behind him. 'I like what I see,' he informed her softly.

Tabby stared up at him with fulminating force, noting the dark shadow of stubble outlining his stubborn jaw line and how that overnight growth enhanced his sheer masculinity. 'But I'm not offering myself.'

'No?' Acheron dipped his handsome head and nibbled at the corner of her inviting mouth, invading with his tongue as soon as she parted her succulent lips. Without further ado, he hauled her up against him, hands weaving across her slender back and then sliding up to glance over the taut peaks of her breasts in a caress that made her shiver.

That single kiss had unholy pulling power. Tabby bargained with herself to continue it. One second, just *one* second more to feel the hungry plunge of his tongue that raised a riot of damp heat low in her body and then his hands, dear heaven, his hands skimming, brushing the tender tips of her breasts before cupping her urgently sensitive flesh. 'No,' she told him shakily.

'No?' Wine-dark eyes glittered down at her, and her swollen mouth ran dry because she wanted another kiss, wanted the wildness she experienced beneath his skilled hands, wanted more with a ferocity that terrified her. Long fingers splayed to her spine, tipping her into revealing contact with the erection that his jeans could not conceal. 'We could have fun for an hour or two.'

'Do I strike you as that easy?' Tabby prompted tightly, outraged by the tone of his proposition. Did he think she was flattered by the idea of being his entertainment for a couple of hours? A quick and easy sexual convenience because there was no more appealing prospect available?

His stunning eyes narrowed. 'I don't make judgements like that about women. I'm not sexist. I enjoy sex. I'm sure you do as well.'

'You're wrong,' she began heatedly, thinking he was little different from the men who, having bought her a drink, had assumed that they were entitled to her body and could not comprehend her reluctance. Sex as a leisure-time pursuit was not her style.

'If you haven't enjoyed sex before then you've been with the wrong men,' Acheron assured her silkily, running a caressing finger along the ripe curve of her lower lip, and the breath feathered deliciously in her throat, a ripple of treacherous, unwelcome response quivering through her slender length.

'You're a class act in the persuasion stakes,' Tabby told him very drily, stepping back out of reach, fighting the unexpected chill of separation from the allure of his warm, vital body. 'But it's wasted on me—though I'm a virgin, I'm well aware that a man will tell you practically anything to get you into bed.'

'A...*virgin*?' Ash echoed in an astonished undertone, disbelief clenching his taut dark features. 'Seriously? Or is that a hook to pull me in deeper?'

Tabby slowly shook her head and then surrendered to laugh out loud. 'You are so suspicious of women it's not real. I don't want to pull you into anything. In fact, I think it would be a very bad idea for us to get that involved.'

'I wasn't thinking of involvement...I was thinking of sex,' Acheron traded smoothly. 'A simple exchange of pleasure.'

Tabby noted the way he even had to separate involvement from the act of sex and registered that he was positively phobic when it came to the concept of commitment. He did not want her to misunderstand what was on offer: a bodily exchange of pleasure, nothing more, no strings whatsoever. 'Goodnight,' she said gruffly, turning on her heel.

'A virgin...*seriously*?' Acheron breathed in her wake, the dark deep richness of his accented drawl vibrating through her in the stillness of the silent apartment.

Tabby turned her head slowly back to him. 'Seriously.'

Acheron frowned, dark brows drawing together, and stared at her, his eyes gleaming golden with curiosity and fascination in the overhead lights. 'But why?'

'I've never wanted to.' *Until now*, a little voice piped up in her brain, for that passionate kiss and the carnal caress of his well-shaped hands had roused more hunger in Tabby than she had ever felt in her life. A fierce physical hunger that she sensed could easily get out of hand.

'You wanted *me, hara mou*...' Acheron murmured with assurance as she walked away from him, blonde hair streaming down her back like a pale flowing river highlighting the curve of her bottom.

Tabby knew she should say nothing, but she couldn't resist the little devil inside herself that he provoked and she turned her head again, succumbing to temptation to murmur softly, 'But obviously…not enough.'

That crack might have affected some men like a challenge, Acheron mused broodingly as he strode back to his room for a cold shower, but he was not one of those men because logic had always ruled his libido. If he slept with her it would clearly get messy, and he hated messy relationships and didn't tolerate them for longer than it took to delete such women's numbers from his phone.

He reminded himself of the dire consequences of his last reckless encounter, and it was even worse that Tabby was still a virgin. He found that hard to credit but could not see any advantage in her telling such a lie. A woman who was still a virgin at twenty-five had to have *very* high expectations of her first lover for why else would she have waited so long? He would not be that man, would never fit that framework or meet the demands she would make. He had been warned and from now on he would keep his distance….

Tabby screened a yawn and settled Amber down on the rug at her feet. So far, it had been a very boring morning. Acheron's lawyer, Stevos, had arrived with a bundle of documents, which had been painstakingly filled in, and now he was engaged in explaining the pre-nuptial contract to her clause by painful clause. Naturally Acheron wanted to protect his wealth, and discussing the terms of divorce before they even got as far as the wedding would have been depressing had she been in love with him, but she wasn't in love with him and couldn't have cared less about his money.

'But I don't need anything like that amount of cash to live on after the divorce,' Tabby protested worriedly. 'I know how to live well on a small budget and even a quarter of that amount would be more than generous.'

'You're supposed to be out for all you can get,' Acheron chipped in helpfully from his restive stance by the window. 'Sign the contract and forget about it. Once you've lived in my world for a while, you'll find your tastes have changed and that you want more.'

Tabby slung him a look of resentment. 'I only want Amber out of this arrangement. I'm not going to turn into a greedy, grasping manipulator overnight either!'

'Mr Dimitrakos simply wants you and the child to enjoy a secure and comfortable future,' the lawyer interposed soothingly.

'No, Mr Dimitrakos wants to buy my loyalty and my loyalty is not for sale!' Tabby replied with spirit. 'I very much appreciate what he is doing to help me keep Amber in my life and the very last thing I will do is take advantage of his generosity in any way. Please accept that.'

'*Sign,*' Acheron slotted with raw impatience. 'This nonsense has taken up enough of my morning.'

'You mustn't forget to be present at the visit from the social worker this afternoon,' Stevos reminded him doggedly.

Stevos planted another document in front of Tabby when she had signed the first. 'It's a standard confidentiality agreement, which will prevent you from talking about the terms of your marriage to anyone outside this office.'

'That it's a big fat fake has to stay a secret,' Acheron interposed bluntly.

Suppressing a sigh, Tabby signed and then glanced up to watch Acheron as he talked to his lawyer in Greek. He was wearing a dark grey suit with a very subtle pinstripe and a purple shirt and he looked…absolutely amazing, as if he had stepped live out of a glossy magazine shoot. Sleek, sophisticated and breathtakingly handsome, he instantly commanded her gaze whenever he came within sight. There was no harm in looking at him and appreciating the view, she told herself ruefully. He was like a beautiful painting she could admire without needing to own, particularly as any woman with ideas of ownership where Acheron Dimitrakos was concerned was, in Tabby's opinion, in for a very rough ride.

They had shared the breakfast table in his dining room earlier that morning but the table was literally *all* they had shared. He had read his newspaper while she tended to Amber and munched toast, struggling to eat as quietly as a mouse in a cat's presence. It had proved neither sociable nor relaxed and she had already decided to eat her meals in the kitchen from now on.

'One of my assistants is going to take you shopping now for a wedding dress,' Acheron divulged as Tabby bent to lift Amber off the rug before she got her little hands on his shoelaces. 'And we will have to engage a nanny to take care of Amber when we're busy.'

Tabby straightened. 'I don't want a wedding dress…or a nanny.'

Scorching dark eyes assailed hers. 'Did I ask for your opinion?'

'No, but you're getting it, no extra charge.'

'A wedding dress is not negotiable.'

'Nothing's negotiable with you!'

Dark eyes flared sensual gold. 'If you were willing to try a little harder to please, you might be surprised,' he murmured huskily.

He was thinking about sex again: she *knew* it by the look in his eyes and the husky tone of his voice. Colour burned up hotly over her cheekbones as she dealt him a quelling glance.

'I'll be honest about this—I don't want to waste a wedding dress on a phony marriage. It just seems wrong,' Tabby admitted, lifting her chin. 'I want to save the white wedding dress for the day I do it for real.'

'Tough,' Acheron responded obstinately, moving closer. 'This may be a rush wedding but I want it to look as normal as possible and few women choose to get married without frills.'

Amber held out her arms to him and smiled.

'Cuddle her,' Tabby instructed, dumping the little girl into his startled arms. 'Practice makes perfect and, just as I have to look convincing at the wedding, you have to look convincing as an adoptive father-to-be this afternoon.'

Amber yanked at Acheron's silk tie with gusto and an appreciative grin suddenly slashed his mouth, shocking both his companions. 'Amber really doesn't give a damn about anything but attention and what amuses her in the moment.'

'A baby's needs are simple,' Tabby agreed wryly, striving not to react to that intensely charismatic smile of his, which made her want to smile back like a dream-struck idiot. Just looking at him, amusement falling from his features, she felt slightly light-headed and her tummy hollowed as if she were travelling downhill at breathtaking speed on a roller coaster. 'The nanny?'

'A necessity when you will have other calls on your time,' Acheron pronounced. 'Be practical.'

Tabby breathed in deep, reluctant to argue with him when the social services interview was to take place within a few hours. She took Amber back into her arms and strapped her into her buggy where the little girl screwed up her face and complained vehemently.

'She knows what she wants,' Acheron remarked. 'You will need to be firm as she gets older.'

'Obviously.'

'And you might find it a challenge to wear that wedding dress for real for some man when you already have a child in tow,' Acheron delivered with lethal cool. '*I* don't date single parents.'

'Tell me something that surprises me,' Tabby urged witheringly. 'You're too selfish, too concerned about protecting your own comfort level.'

'I just respect my limitations.'

'Nonsense. You can't stand the idea of having to

consider someone else's needs before your own,' Tabby traded.

'So, what am I doing now in marrying you?' Acheron demanded curtly.

'You're righting the wrong you committed a couple of months ago when you refused to be Amber's guardian and no doubt that makes you feel so unselfish and perfect you think you're one hell of a guy!'

Listening to that exchange, Stevos was staring in shock at Tabby and her colour was high when she released the brake on the buggy and wheeled it out of the door.

Acheron's PA, Sharma, greeted her in the outer office and took her straight out to a limo for the shopping trip. Tabby was surprised to be taken to an exclusive and very fashionable wedding boutique rather than a department store, but appreciated that with the time available it would be a challenge to come up with a sophisticated dress that fitted the bill. While Sharma played with Amber, Tabby tried on gowns, finally selecting the least fussy available and choosing the accessories suggested by the attentive proprietor. That achieved, she returned to Acheron's apartment and rang Jack to tell him that she was getting married and to invite him to the civil ceremony the following day.

'Is this a joke?' Jack asked.

'No. It is kind of sudden but I know exactly what I'm doing. Acheron wants to adopt Amber with me.'

'You've kept this very quiet. How long have you been seeing him for?' Jack enquired ruefully.

'A while. I didn't know it was going to turn serious or I'd have mentioned it sooner,' Tabby fibbed, wishing she could just have told the truth.

'It'll solve all your problems,' Jack pronounced with satisfaction. 'I've been really worried about you and Amber.'

Acheron turned up just in time for the interview with the social worker and swiftly proved a dab hand at twisting the truth, contriving to make it sound as if they had known each other far longer than they had. The older woman was so palpably impressed by Acheron and his incredible apartment that she asked few searching questions.

An hour later Tabby was feeding Amber and stealing bites from her own meal in the kitchen when Acheron appeared in the doorway, his expression thunderous. He swept up the highchair with Amber in it and turned on his heel.

'What on earth are you doing?' Tabby cried, racing after him.

Acheron set the chair down at one end of the dining table. 'We eat in here together. You do not eat in the kitchen like a member of my staff. That will not support the impression of a normal married couple.'

'I shouldn't think any of your staff could care less where we eat!' Tabby replied.

'But you need to be more cautious about appearances,' Acheron spelled out the warning grimly. 'Any one of my staff could sell a story to the tabloids and blow a massive hole in our pretence of being a couple.'

Tabby fell still. 'I never thought of that. Can't you trust your employees?'

'Most of them but there's always a rotten apple somewhere in the barrel,' Acheron answered with cynical cool.

Tabby nodded and returned to the kitchen to fetch her meal. He thought of every pitfall from every possible angle and it shook her that he had evidently already suffered that kind of betrayal from someone close to him. It was little wonder that he continually expected the worst from people, she reflected ruefully.

'Why were you eating in the kitchen?' he enquired as she settled at the table.

'I know you like your own space,' Tabby said quickly.

'You're not comfortable eating with me. I noticed that in the restaurant the first night,' Acheron commented, resting level dark eyes on her rising colour. 'You'll have to get over that.'

'Yes, but it was a strain that first night,' Tabby admitted, grudgingly opting for honesty. 'I couldn't read the menu because my French isn't up to it. I didn't even know which cutlery to use.'

A stab of remorse pierced Acheron. It had not even occurred to him that she might feel out of her depth at his favourite restaurant. 'Cutlery isn't important, *hara mou*—'

'Believe me, it *is* when you don't know which utensil to use.'

'In future, *ask*.' Acheron compressed his wide, sensual mouth, irritated that he had been so inconsiderate of the differences between them. 'I'm not…sensitive. I won't pick up on things like that unless you warn me. By the way, Sharma has engaged last night's nanny to work for us. I've also secured permission for us to take Amber abroad.'

'Abroad?' Tabby exclaimed. 'What are you talking about?'

'We're heading to Italy after the wedding. I have a house there. It will be easier to keep up the newly married act without an audience of friends and acquaintances looking on,' Acheron pointed out with irreproachable practicality.

Tabby woke early the next morning. Well, it was her wedding day even though it bore no resemblance to the very special event she had once dreamt the occasion would be. For a start, Sonia would not be there to play bridesmaid as the two women had always assumed she would, and momentarily Tabby's eyes stung with tears because sometimes the pain of losing her best friend felt like a wound that would never heal. She reminded herself that she still had Jack, but Jack was a man of few words and his girlfriend, Emma, was uneasy about his friendship with Tabby. As a result Tabby kept contact with Jack to the minimum. With a sigh, she rolled out of bed to go and tend to Amber and get dressed.

The nanny, Melinda, was in Amber's bedroom. Tabby had forgotten about the nanny, forgotten that she was no longer the only person available to care for the little girl, and Amber was already bathed, dressed and fed. A little pang of regret assailed Tabby because she had always enjoyed giving Amber her first peaceful feed of the day. But Sonia's daughter still greeted her with uninhibited love and affection, and Tabby buried her nose in the little girl's sweet-smelling hair and breathed deep, reminding herself why she was marrying Acheron and meeting his every demand. Amber was worth almost any sacrifice, she conceded feelingly.

The ceremony was to be held at an exclusive castle hotel, and Tabby was amazed at how much it had been possible to arrange at such speed. Then she reminded herself that Acheron's wealth would have ensured special attention and she scolded herself for being so naive.

Sharma had arranged for a hairstylist and a make-up artist to attend her at the apartment, and Tabby hoped that their professional skill would give her at least a hint of the glossy sophistication that Acheron's female companions usually exuded. As quick as she thought that, she wondered why his opinion should matter to her. Was it simply a matter of pride?

Sharma helped lace Tabby into her dress while the stylist adjusted the short flirty veil attached to the circlet of fresh flowers attached to Tabby's hair.

'With those flowers on your head you look like the Queen of Summer…' Sharma burbled enthusiastically. 'Mr Dimitrakos will be blown away.'

It dawned on Tabby for the first time that she was dealing with someone who thought she was about to attend a genuine wedding and she flushed with discomfiture, quite certain that the last thing Acheron would be was 'blown away'.

'And watching the boss go to so much trouble to get married in such a hurry is *so* romantic,' Sharma continued. 'I used to think he was so… er, cold, no offence intended…and then I saw him with the baby and realised how wrong I was. Of course fatherhood does change a man…'

And Tabby registered that Sharma had, not unnaturally, added two and two to make five in her assumption that Acheron was Amber's father. 'Actually, Amber is the daughter of my late best friend and Acheron's cousin,' she explained, deeming it wiser to put the other woman right on that score.

Grim-faced, Acheron paced while he awaited the arrival of the bridal car. He was very tense. It might be a fake wedding but with the arrival of his stepmother, Ianthe, and two of her adult children along with several good friends, it felt unnervingly real and he was already fed up with making polite conversation and pretending to be a happy bridegroom. Unhappily, a wedding without guests would not have been a very convincing affair, he reminded himself impatiently, and at least the woman whose attendance would have been least welcome had failed to show up. Stationed by the window of the function room adorned with flowers for the ceremony, he watched as a limousine embellished with white ribbons that fluttered in the breeze drew up at the hotel entrance.

Tabby stepped out in a sleek bell of rustling white fabric and petticoats, little shoulders bare, her veil and glorious streamers of golden-blonde hair blowing back from her oval face. Acheron's expressive mouth hardened even more, a nerve pulling taut at the corner of his lips. She looked as dainty and delicate as a doll and utterly ravishing, he noted in exasperation, cursing his all-too-male response to so feminine and alluring an image. Tabby didn't just clean up well, in Stevos's parlance; she cleaned up spectacular, Acheron conceded wryly, only absently registering the emergence of the new nanny clutching Amber, who was looking similarly festive in a candy-pink dress and matching hairband.

Tabby was guided straight into the ceremony where music was already playing. Her apprehensive glance took in the sea of faces and then lodged on Acheron and stayed there as if pad-locked. *Whoosh!* She could feel all her defences being sucked away by the pure power of his com-pelling presence. He stared back at her, making no pretence of looking forward to the registrar, his stunning dark eyes golden and bright as sun-light in his lean face and so gorgeous he made something low in her body clench tight like a fist. Knees a tad wobbly, she walked down the short aisle between the seated guests and stilled by his side, the words of the brief ceremony washing over her while she frantically reminded herself that finding Acheron attractive was a one-way trip to disaster and not to be risked lest it should somehow threaten Amber's future as well.

He slid a ring onto her finger and she did the same for him. Afterwards, he retained his grip on her hand, ignoring her attempt to tug gently free, and suddenly there was a crowd of people round them murmuring congratulations, and in-troductions were being made.

His stepmother was a decorative blonde with a shrill voice and she had a son and a daughter by her side, both of whom seemed rather in awe of

Acheron, which gave Tabby the impression that he had never been a true part of his father's family. Jack appeared with his girlfriend, Emma, and the other woman was friendlier than Tabby had ever seen her. Tabby chatted at length to Jack and turned only to find Acheron studying her, his handsome mouth compressed.

'Who was that?'

'Jack's an old friend and the only person I invited,' she proclaimed defensively.

'How much did you tell him?' Acheron enquired grimly.

'I told him nothing,' Tabby responded, wondering what his problem was. 'He thinks this is all for real.'

Drinks were being poured and toasts made by the time a tall, curvy brunette in a sapphire-blue suit swept into the room without warning.

Someone close to Tabby vented a groan. The brunette marched up to them like a woman on a mission and shot an outraged look at Acheron's stepmother, Ianthe. 'Mother, how could you take part in this insane charade when it goes against *my* interests?' she demanded loudly. 'I should have been the bride here today!'

'Let's not go there, Kasma,' her brother, Simeon, advised sheepishly. 'We're here to celebrate Ash's wedding, and I know you don't want to spoil the day by creating a scene.'

'Don't I?' Kasma struck an attitude, furious dark eyes glittering bright. She was a very beautiful woman with a great figure, a perfect face and a torrent of long dark hair, Tabby noted in a daze of agitation. 'Tell me, what has *she* got that I haven't, Acheron?' she demanded in a fierce tone of accusation.

Amber was starting to cry and Tabby took the opportunity to step out of the drama to join Melinda, the nanny, at the back of the room. After all, family squabbles and bitter ex-lovers were none of her business. Had Acheron had an affair with his stepsister? By the looks of it, it had been a rash move to utilise his charisma within the family circle, and she could understand why he had said on the first day that they met at his office that he had *no* family. His late father's family spoke to Acheron as politely as the strangers they so clearly were. Evidently he had never lived with them, which made her wonder who he *had* lived with when he was younger because Tabby was convinced she remembered his very famous mother's death being announced on television while she herself was still only a child.

Tabby took Amber into the baby-changing room, thinking that the histrionic Kasma would, with a little luck, be gone by the time she returned to sit down to a late and much-needed lunch.

But she was to have no such luck. No sooner had she finished undressing Amber than the door opened to frame Kasma's lush shape. 'Is that child Ash's?' she asked drily.

Tabby changed Amber, who was squirming like mad and craning her neck to look at the visitor. 'No.'

'I didn't think so,' Kasma said snidely. 'Ash has never been the daddy type.'

Exasperation kindling, Tabby straightened her shoulders and turned her head. 'Look, I don't know you and I'm busy here—'

'You know why Ash married you, don't you?' the brunette continued thinly. '*I* should have been

Ash's bride. No one understands him as well as I do. Unfortunately for all three of us, he's too stubborn and proud to accept being forced to do what he should have done long ago.'

'I don't need to know what you're talking about,' Tabby told her uncomfortably. 'It's really none of my business.'

'How can you say that when by marrying Ash you're winning him a fortune?' Kasma demanded resentfully, her mother's vocal shrillness feeding into her sharp tone. 'According to the terms of his father's will if he stayed single until the end of the year he would lose half of *his* company to *my* family! And, of course, anyone who knows how Ash feels about his company would know that he would do virtually *anything* to protect it... even marry a totally unsuitable nobody from nowhere to maintain the status quo!'

CHAPTER FIVE

KASMA'S ACCUSATION RANG in Tabby's ears like a nasty echo during the flight to Italy. After the brunette's departure, lunch had proceeded quietly but Tabby had not had the advantage of a private moment in which to question Acheron. She had intended to raise the subject during the flight but Melinda was looking after Amber at the back of the cabin and she did not feel that she could speak freely.

Was it possible that Acheron had had a far more self-serving motive to marry than he had admitted? Tabby deemed it perfectly possible when she compared his refusal of all responsibility for Amber only months earlier with his sudden change of heart. Why on earth hadn't she been more suspicious of that rapid turnaround of his? He had to think she was as dumb as a rock, she thought painfully, feeling betrayed not only by his lack of honesty but also by her own gullibility. What terms had been included in his father's will? How could he possibly lose half of a company that belonged to him? And if Kasma's information was correct, why hadn't Acheron simply told Tabby the truth?

And the answer to that question could only be *power*, Tabby reflected with steadily mounting anger. As long as Tabby had believed that Acheron was doing her a favour for Amber's sake she had been willing to meet his every demand because she had been grateful to him, believing that he was making a big sacrifice even if theirs was only a fake marriage. But what if it wasn't like that at all? What if Acheron Dimitrakos had needed a conformable wife just as much as she needed the support and stability that would enable her to adopt Amber? That very much changed the picture and made them equals. But Acheron had never been prepared to treat Tabby as an equal. Acheron preferred to dictate and demand, not persuade and compromise. Well, those days were gone if Kasma had told her the truth…

'You're very quiet,' Acheron commented in the car driving them through the Tuscan countryside.

She had changed out of her wedding gown before leaving London, and he had felt weirdly disappointed when he saw her wearing the violet dress he had personally chosen for her in London instead. The fabric and long sleeves were too heavy for a warmer climate and there was a flush of pink on her face in spite of the air conditioning. The colour, however, brought out the remarkable shade of her eyes and somehow accentuated the succulent fullness of her pink mouth.

Acheron breathed in slow and deep, dropped his gleaming gaze only for it to lodge on a slender knee and the soft pale skin beneath, which only made him wonder if her skin would feel as silky to the touch as it looked. He gritted his teeth, cursing his high-voltage libido. It had never once crossed his mind until now that, even with the options he had, a platonic relationship might still be a challenge, but evidently he was suffering from sexual frustration. Why else would he find her so appealing?

'I'm enjoying the views,' Tabby proclaimed stiltedly, so angry with him that she had to bite her lower lip before she started an argument while still trapped in the car with him. 'Where exactly are we going?'

'A villa in the hills. Like most of my properties it once belonged to my mother but I had it renovated last year.'

Despite her anger, curiosity stirred in Tabby. 'Your mother died when you were still quite young, didn't she?' she remarked.

His lean bronzed features clenched hard, dark golden eyes screening. 'Yes.'

The wall of reserve he used as a shield cast a forbidding shadow over his expressionless face. 'I lost my parents quite young too,' Tabby told him, rushing to fill the uneasy silence with an innate sensitivity towards his feelings that annoyed her. 'I went into foster care. That's where I met Jack and Amber's mum, Sonia.'

'I didn't realise you'd been in foster care,' Acheron breathed flatly, well aware she would not have had the escape route from that lifestyle that had eventually been granted by his inherited wealth.

'Well...' Tabby responded awkwardly, colliding with impenetrable midnight eyes heavily fringed by spiky black lashes and fighting a sensation of falling…and falling…and falling. 'They weren't the happiest years of my life but there were some good times. The last foster home I was in was the best and at least the three of us were together there.'

That appeared to be the end of that conversation as Acheron compressed his lips in grim silence while Tabby fought that light-headed sensation and struggled to focus on her anger. So, Acheron Dimitrakos was gorgeous and he kept on making her hormones sit up and take notice but he was also a skilled manipulator and deceiver and only a complete fool would forget the fact. In addition, it had not escaped her notice that he really wasn't interested in learning anything about her background and who she was as a person. But then had he ever seen her as a person in her own right? Or simply as someone he could easily use?

The car turned off the road and purred up a sloping driveway to the very large ochre-coloured stone building sprawling across the top of the hill. Tabby had to tense her lower lip to prevent her mouth from dropping open in comical awe because what he called a villa *she* would have called a palace. A fountain was playing a rainbow of sparkling water droplets down into a circular pool in the centre of a paved frontage already embellished with giant stone pots of glorious flowers. As she climbed out into the early evening sunshine, a flicker of movement from a shrubbery attracted her attention and a white peacock strutted out, unfurling his pristine feathers. The light caught his plumage as he unfurled it like a magnificent silver lace fan. The peacock posed, head high, one foot lifted, his confidence supreme in spite of his aloneness.

'You remind me of that bird,' Tabby muttered as the car carrying Amber and her nanny with the bodyguards drew up behind them.

Acheron raised an ebony brow enquiringly.

Embarrassed, Tabby shrugged. 'Never mind. Could we have a word in private?' she asked then.

'Of course,' he said without expression, but she didn't miss the frowning glance he shot in her direction as she moved to speak to Amber and her nanny. The little girl was fast asleep though, and a last feed and an early night were clearly what she most needed after a long and exhausting day.

The hall of the villa was breathtaking. Gleaming stretches of marble flooring ran below the arches that separated the reception areas. Tabby had never seen so many different shades of white utilised in a decor or anything so impractical for a household with a child in tow. Of course they would not be staying for long, she reminded herself, and Amber wasn't yet mobile so all the sharp-edged glass coffee tables and stylishly sited sculptural pieces on pedestals would scarcely endanger her.

'Very impressive,' she pronounced while Melinda followed the housekeeper up the wrought-iron and marble staircase.

'I have a few calls to make,' Acheron informed her and he was already swinging away, a tall, broad-shouldered male in a beautifully cut light-weight suit made of a fine fabric that gleamed in the light flooding through the windows.

'We have to talk...'

Over the years, far too many women had fired that same phrase at Acheron and had followed it with dramatic scenes and demands for more attention that he found abhorrent. His powerful

frame tensed, his lean, strong face shuttering.
'Not now…later.'

'Yes…*now*,' Tabby emphasised without hesitation, violet eyes shimmering with anger, for
she was not going to allow him to rudely brush
her off as if she were the nobody from nowhere
and of no account that Kasma had labelled her.
If she toed his line and treated him like a superior being she would soon be thinking the same
thing about herself.

'What is this about?' Acheron enquired coldly.

Tabby walked very deliberately out of the hall
into the area furnished with incredibly opulent
white sofas and slowly turned round, slim shoulders straight, chin lifted. 'Is it true that to retain
ownership of your company your father's will
required you to take a wife before the end of the
year?'

His stubborn jaw line clenched. 'Where did you
get that story from?' he asked grittily and then he
released his breath with a measured hiss of com-
prehension. 'Kasma…*right*?'

'It's true, then,' Tabby gathered in furious disbelief. 'She told me the truth.'

'The terms of my father's will are nothing to do with you,' Acheron stated with chilling bite, his dark eyes deep and cold as the depths of the ocean.

But Tabby was in no mood to be intimidated. 'How dare you say that when getting married must've suited you every bit as much as it suited me? Didn't you think I deserved to know that?'

Acheron gritted his even white teeth together in a visible act of restraint. 'What difference can it possibly make to you?'

'I think it makes a *huge* difference!' Tabby slung back at him, violet eyes darkening with seething resentment. 'You made me feel as if you were doing me an enormous favour for Amber's benefit.'

'And wasn't I?' Acheron slotted in, utilising a tone that was not calculated to soothe wounded feelings.

'And you can stop being so rude right now!' Tabby launched at him, that derisive tone and superior appraisal of his lashing her like an offensive assault. 'Yes, Acheron, it *is* rude to interrupt and even more rude to look at me as if I'm some bug on the ground at your feet! I was completely honest with you but you, and no doubt your lawyer, deceived me.'

Eyes smouldering gold, Acheron was having trouble holding on to his temper. 'How you were deceived? I did exactly as I promised. I married you, I helped you to lodge an adoption application and I have ensured your future security. A lot of women would kill for one half of what I'm giving you!'

Her slender hands closed into irate fists. She wanted to pummel him as he stood there, the king of all he surveyed, cocooned from ordinary mortals and decent moral tenets by a level of wealth and success she could barely imagine. 'You are so arrogant, so hateful sometimes I want to hit you and I'm not a violent person!' Tabby hastened to declare in her own defence. 'Do you honestly not understand why I'm angry? I was frank with you. There were no lies, no pretences, no evasions. I believe I deserve the same respect from you.'

His wide, sensual mouth curled. 'This doesn't feel like respect.'

'Is this how you normally deal with an argument?'

'I don't have arguments with people,' Acheron responded levelly.

'Only because people probably spend all their time trying to please and flatter you, not because they always agree with you!' Tabby snapped back in vexation. 'For someone who appears very confrontational, you're actually avoiding the issue and refusing to respond to my natural annoyance.'

'I don't wish to prolong this argument, nor do I see anything natural about your annoyance,' Acheron admitted curtly. 'I don't make a habit of confiding in people. I'm a very private individual, and my father's will certainly falls into the confidential category.'

'I had the right to know that I didn't need to be grateful and submit to your every demand because you were getting even more out of this marriage than I was!' Tabby condemned, refusing to be sidetracked by a red herring like his reserve. 'You used my ignorance like a weapon against me!'

'The will was a matter of business and was of

no conceivable interest to you,' Acheron stated in a raw undertone.

'Don't talk nonsense. Of course it was of interest to me that you had as much need to get married as I did!' she flashed back at him. 'It levels the playing field.'

'As far as I'm concerned, there *is* no playing field because this is not a game!' Acheron countered angrily. 'I married you and now that you're my wife, you're trying to take advantage of your position.'

Her violet eyes widened and she planted her tiny hands on her hips, just like a miniature fishwife getting ready to do battle, he decided, torn between grudging amusement and exasperation. 'Take advantage? How am I taking advantage? By standing up to you for once? By daring to state *my* side of the case?' she hissed back at him with simmering rancour.

Acheron strode forward, planted two hands over hers and hauled her up into the air before she could even guess his intention. He held her there, entrapped. 'You don't have a side of the case to argue, *moraki mou*—'

Enraged by his behaviour, Tabby glowered down at him. 'If you don't put me down, I'll kick you!' she launched at him furiously.

In response, Acheron banded her closely to his big powerful length, ensuring that her legs were as trapped as her hands. Dark golden eyes fringed by heavy black lashes held hers fast. 'There will be *no* kicking, *no* hitting, *no* bad language—'

'Says who?' Tabby bit out between gritted teeth.

'Your husband.' Acheron frowned as though that aspect had only just occurred to him and he was as much amused as irritated by the reality.

It was as if she were a firework and he had lit her up inside. Rage blazed through Tabby. 'You are *not* my husband!'

Unholy amusement lit Acheron's eyes, whipping up the lighter tones she had noticed before and giving him an extraordinary appeal that made her mouth run dry and her tummy perform acrobatics. 'Then what am I?'

'A rat with a marriage certificate!' Tabby snapped at him informatively.

Acheron gave her a look of mock sympathy. '*Your* rat because you're stuck with me.'

'Put…me…down!' Tabby ground out fiercely. 'Or you'll regret it!'

'No, I much prefer this set-up to you shouting at me from across the room.'

'I was not shouting!'

'You were shouting,' Acheron repeated steadily. 'That is not how I conduct disputes.'

'I don't give a monkey's about how you like to conduct your disputes!' Tabby fired back.

It was those sparkling eyes, that incredibly succulent and inviting mouth of hers, Acheron mused abstractedly, conscious that she somehow hauled fiercely on every libidinous hormone he possessed and fired him up like a horny teenager. He didn't understand it, didn't care, didn't think he needed to, but without conscious volition he drew that tempting mouth up to his and crushed it under his, and the taste of her was as rich and fragrant and luscious as juicy strawberries on a summer day.

'No… No,' Tabby's dismayed objections, voiced as much to her wayward self as to him, were swallowed up by the hot, hungry pressure of his erotically charged mouth on hers.

Nobody had ever kissed Tabby as he did with all the passion of the volatile nature he kept under wraps, but which she sensed every time she was with him. He demanded and teased and the force of his sensual lips on hers followed by the invasive plunge of his tongue was unbelievably exciting and sexy.

He was very, *very* sexy, she acknowledged dimly, as if it was an excuse, and as he hoisted her higher to get a better grip on her slight body he let go of her hands and, instead of using them to get free of his hold, she balanced one on a broad shoulder and delved the fingers of the other into the springy, luxuriant depths of his black hair. With a guttural sound low in his throat he brought her down on something soft and yielding and then sealed her fast to the hard, driving length of his powerful frame.

And even as a faint current of alarm blipped somewhere in the back of Tabby's head she was aware of how much she loved feeling his strong, muscular body over and on hers. In fact, her every skin cell was leaping and bouncing with pent-up energy long before his fingers closed over the slight thrust of her achingly sensitive breast, and she strained up breathless and bound by a new tide of sensation. Indeed, desire had infiltrated her with such powerful effect that she scarcely knew what she was doing any more. Nothing had ever felt more necessary; nothing had ever felt more thrilling than the hot, hungry stimulation of his mouth and his hands. Spasms of excitement were quivering through her in a gathering storm. But then other sounds suddenly cancelled out those physical responses: a stifled gasp linked to the rattle of china and the sound of hastily receding footsteps.

'My goodness, what was that?' Tabby exclaimed, dragging her mouth from beneath his to find that she was lying on a sofa beneath him. *Beneath him*, her brain repeated, and her body went into panic mode when she collided with smouldering dark golden eyes and pushed at his shoulders, wriggling out from under his weight at frantic, feverish speed.

'Let's go to bed,' Acheron husked, closing long brown fingers over hers.

And it's just that simple and casual for him, she

told herself angrily, furious that she had not contrived to resist him. She perched at the far end of the sofa, smoothing her tumbled blonde hair back from her brow, a slight tremor in her hands and her face so hot with mortification she could have boiled eggs on it. 'No, let's not…it would mess up things.'

'The bed would be more comfortable than the sofa,' Acheron declared single-mindedly.

'I'm not talking about *where*…I'm saying *no*, we're not going to do that!' Tabby slung back at him in frustration, wincing at the nagging bite of separation from his lean, hard body, fighting the ache of longing between her thighs with defiant determination. No way was she planning to be one more in a no doubt long line of easy women for Acheron, a mere female body to scratch an itch for a male unaccustomed to doing without sexual satisfaction.

Acheron sprawled back at the other end of the sofa, long powerful thighs spread so that she noticed, really couldn't help noticing, that that little tussle with her body had seriously aroused his. Her face burned even hotter and her tummy hollowed just looking at the prominent bulge at his pelvis, reactions to a physical craving she had never experienced before assailing her in an unwelcome wave.

All of a sudden and no thanks to Acheron for the lesson, she was realising why she was still a virgin. No other man had ever attracted her enough to make her drop her guard and yearn for sex. Sex, yes, that was all it would be, straightforward, unvarnished sex, not something a sensible woman would crave, and she was very sensible, wasn't she? *Wasn't she?* It really bothered her that even while thinking along those lines and carefully realigning her defences she was still fully engaged in appreciating the pure male beauty of Acheron's lean bronzed face and long, powerful body.

'You want me,' Acheron breathed a little raggedly. 'I want you.'

'Weird, isn't it…? I mean, we can't even be civil to each other,' Tabby pronounced shakily, still as out of breath as he was, recalling that wild entanglement and the fierce need he had sent powering through her and then suppressing the uncomfortable memory before standing up, smoothing down her dress with careful hands.

'Yet you burn me up, *hara mou*,' Acheron breathed huskily, springing upright with easy grace.

Tabby turned her head away. 'Let's not talk about that…you and me? It would be a very bad idea. We have as much in common as a cat and a dog. I'd like to see my room,' she completed, moving back with determination towards the hall.

'I'll show you. We've frightened off the staff,' Acheron volunteered with an unconcerned laugh. 'I think that noise was someone bringing us coffee and we were seen.'

'Yes, I can imagine what they saw,' Tabby cut in stiltedly, wishing he would drop the subject.

'Well, that's at least one person who will believe that we're genuine honeymooners,' Acheron replied nonchalantly, refusing to take the hint as he led the way up the marble staircase.

'But we're *not*,' she reminded him doggedly.

'You're not a very flexible personality, are you?'

'You'd roll me out like pastry if I was,' Tabby

quipped. 'I'm still mad at you, Acheron. You took advantage of my ignorance.'

'I'm an alpha male, programmed at birth to take advantage,' Acheron pointed out with unapologetic cool. 'But you called me on it, which I wasn't expecting.'

He pushed open double doors at the end of the corridor and exposed a small hall containing two doors. 'That's my room.' He thrust open one door and then the second. 'And yours…'

Tabby worried at her full lower lip. 'Do we have to be so close?'

'I don't sleepwalk,' Acheron murmured silkily. 'But you're very welcome if you choose to visit.'

'I won't be doing that.' Tabby strolled in the big room, glancing into the en suite that led off and then into a dressing room to slide open a wardrobe, only to frown at the garments packed within. 'Didn't your last girlfriend take her clothes with her?'

'Those are yours. I ordered them,' Acheron explained. 'You'll need summer clothes here.'

Tabby spun back to study him with simmering violet eyes. 'I'm not a dress-up doll.'

'But you know that all I want to do is *undress* you, *moraki mou.*'

Tabby went pink again and compressed her lips.

'You blush like a bonfire,' Acheron remarked with sudden amusement as he strode off to make use of another door on the opposite side of the room that evidently led to his suite.

Tabby thought about turning the lock and then decided it would be petty, for surprisingly on that level she trusted him and had no fear that he might try to take what she was not prepared to offer. If she withstood his appeal, she was quite certain he would withstand hers and find some far more amusing and experienced quarry to pursue. Unfortunately, she didn't like the idea of him with another woman in the slightest and she told herself off for that because she knew she couldn't have it both ways. Either they were together or they were not; there was no halfway stage to explore.

Acheron stripped off for a cold shower. He was still ragingly erect and wondering when a woman had last turned him down. He couldn't remember, and the shock of Tabby's steely resolve still rankled. But it was a timely warning to steer clear, he reflected impatiently, his sensual mouth twisting as he stifled the urge to fantasise about having her tiny body wrapped round him while he satisfied them both. If she attached *that* much importance to sex, he definitely didn't want to get involved because sex meant no more to him than an appetite that required regular satisfaction.

Tabby rifled through the new wardrobe he had acquired for her without even mentioning his intent. She tugged out a long cotton dress that looked cool and, more importantly, covered up anything that she imagined a man might find tempting. If he kept his hands off her, she would keep her hands off him. She worried at her lower lip with her teeth. She had wanted to rip his clothes off him on that sofa, and the incredible strength of the hunger he had awakened still shocked her in retrospect. But nothing more was going to happen, *nothing*, she stressed inwardly with more force than cool. She could handle him, of course she could. He might be a very rich, very good-looking and very manipulative male but she had always had a good gut instinct about how best to look after herself.

Buoyed up by that knowledge, Tabby got changed, freshened up and went off to find out where the nursery had been set up.

CHAPTER SIX

'IT'S TIME YOU told me something about yourself,' Acheron declared, settling back into his seat and cradling his wineglass in one elegant hand.

Tabby was ill at ease. The grand dining room and the table festooned with flowers and fancy dishes for the first meal they were to share as a married couple made her feel like Cinderella arriving at the ball without a prince on hand to claim her. He had watched her watching him to see which cutlery to use, and the awareness had embarrassed her, making her wish that she had never confessed her ignorance. 'What sort of something?'

Acheron raised an ebony brow. 'Let's be basic—your background?'

He was so relaxed that he infuriated her, sheathed in tight faded denim jeans and a black shirt left undone at the throat. She had assumed he would dress up for dinner much as aristocrats seemed to do on television shows and, if she was honest, that was probably why she had picked the long dress. But instead of dressing up, Acheron had dressed *down* and, maddeningly, he still looked amazing, black hair curling a little from the shower, stubborn jaw line slightly rough with dark stubble, lustrous dark eyes pinned to her with uncompromising intensity and she couldn't read him, couldn't read him at all, hadn't a clue what he was thinking about.

'My background's not pretty,' she warned him.

He shrugged a shoulder in dismissal of that objection.

Tabby clenched her teeth and stiffened her backbone. 'I imagine my conception was an accident. My parents weren't married. My mother once told me they were going to give me up for adoption until they discovered that having a child meant they could get better housing and more benefits out of the welfare system. They were both druggies.'

Acheron no longer seemed quite so relaxed and he sat forward with a sudden frown. *'Addicts?'*

'I warned you that it wasn't pretty. Their drug

of choice was whatever was cheapest and most easily available. They weren't parents in the normal sense of the word, and I don't think they were even that keen on each other because they had terrible fights. I was simply the child who lived with them,' Tabby proffered tightly. 'And I got in the way…frequently because children have needs and they didn't meet them.'

Acheron forced his shoulders back into the chair, his astonishment at what she had told him concealed by his impassive expression. He almost told her then and there in a revelation that would have been unprecedented for him that they had much more in common than a cat and a dog.

'Have you heard enough?' Tabby enquired hopefully.

'I want to hear it *all*,' Acheron contradicted levelly, slowly comprehending the base level of painful isolation and insecurity from which that chippy, aggressive manner of hers had undoubtedly been forged. Tabby had been forced at an early age to learn to fight for her survival, and that he understood.

'I was the kid in the wrong clothes at school…

when they got me there, which wasn't very often. Then my father started to take me with him as a lookout when he burgled houses,' she confided flatly, hating every word she was telling him but somehow needing him to know that she could handle her troubled, crime-infested childhood and indeed had moved far beyond it. 'Social Services got involved when he was caught in the act and eventually, because I was missing so much school and my parents were incapable of looking after me properly, I was put into care.'

'As was I,' Acheron admitted gruffly. 'I was ten years old. What age were you?'

Tabby stared back at him wide-eyed. '*You*... were in care? But your parents must have been *so* wealthy.'

'Which doesn't necessarily mean that they were any more responsible than yours,' Acheron pointed out drily. 'Believe me, my mother's money didn't protect me, although it did protect *her* until the day she died from an overdose. Her lawyers rushed her out of the country before she could be prosecuted for neglecting me.'

'What about your father?' Tabby prompted

sickly, still shaken and appalled that he, who seemed so very assured and rich and protected, could ever have lived within the care system as she had. All at once she felt guilty about the assumptions she had made.

'His marriage to my mother only lasted about five minutes. When she got bored with him she told him that the child she was expecting—*me*—was the child of her previous lover...and he believed her,' Acheron explained flatly. 'He couldn't have afforded to fight her for custody in any case. I met him for the first time when I was in my twenties. He came to see me in London because a relative of his had noticed how very alike we looked in a newspaper photograph.'

'So what did your mother do with you?' Tabby asked, sipping at her glass of water.

'Very little. The trust who controlled her millions paid for a squad of carers to look after her and keep her worst excesses out of the newspapers. She was addicted to drugs too,' Acheron divulged tautly. 'But once I was no longer a baby none of her staff had a direct mandate to look after me, and my mother was, all too frequently, high as a kite. So I was left to my own devices, which eventually attracted the attention of the authorities. I had no other relatives to take responsibility for me.'

Painfully aware of the grim memories shadowing his eyes and the sad knowledge that his father could not have been waiting in the wings to take charge of him, Tabby stretched her hand across the table without even thinking about it and rested it down on his, where his long, elegant fingers were braced on the tablecloth. 'I'm sorry.'

His arrogant dark head came up at a combative angle even as he lifted his hand to close it round hers, glancing down at their linked hands in virtual bewilderment as if he couldn't quite work out how that connection had happened. Dark colour crawled up to accentuate the high cheekbones that gave his face such strength and definition. 'Why would you be sorry? I imagine I got off lighter than you. I suspect you were physically mistreated...?'

Her oval face froze. 'Yes,' she almost whispered in confirmation.

'I only met with physical abuse *after* I entered

the care system. I was an obnoxious little brat by then, semi-feral and may well have deserved what I got,' Acheron volunteered between gritted teeth.

'No child deserves pain,' Tabby argued.

'I endured two years of complete hell and innumerable different homes until my mother died and the trustees rescued me. I was sent off to boarding school for what remained of my childhood.'

Tabby's heart squeezed tight and her throat thickened at the awareness that just like her he had grown up knowing nothing of the love and security of a happy home and committed parents. She had been *so* wrong about him and it shamed her that she had been so biased purely because his late mother had been a famous Greek heiress. 'You never forget it…how powerless and lost you feel,' she framed unevenly.

Acheron looked across the table at her, his stunning dark golden eyes glittering. 'You leave it behind you, move on,' he told her squarely, suddenly releasing her hand.

'Yes, but it's always there somewhere in the back of your mind.' Starstruck even as she yanked her hand back, she collided with his eyes and the rare warmth of connection there and it made her feel not as if she was falling but instead flying high as a bird, breathless and thrilled.

'Not if you discipline yourself,' Acheron asserted smoothly.

'Tell me about your father's will,' Tabby urged, already dreading the return of the cold reserve that was beginning to clench his lean, darkly handsome features again.

'Some other time. We've raked over enough personal stuff for one evening…surely?' A sleek black emphatic brow lifted, the force of his will bearing down on her from the lambent glow of his beautiful lustrous dark eyes.

And Tabby, who was usually like a nail stuck to a magnet when in the grip of curiosity, quelled her desire to know more, conceding that, for a male as famously reticent as he was, he had been remarkably frank with her when he hadn't needed to be, for she knew of no stories referring to his dysfunctional upbringing that had ever appeared in the media. She swallowed back her questions and lifted a fork to attack the dessert that had been brought to the table.

'I'm crazy about meringue,' she confided. 'And this is perfectly cooked, crunchy on the outside, soft inside.'

A flashing smile crossed his wide, sensual mouth. 'A little like you, then? All fight on the surface and then all tender when it comes to another woman's child?'

In receipt of that rare smile, she felt her heart race. 'I only want Amber to have all the things I never had.'

'An admirable ambition. I've never had the desire to reproduce,' Acheron admitted, watching the tip of her tongue flick out to catch a tiny white crumb of meringue that could not possibly have tasted any sweeter than her lush mouth. Just like that he was hard as a rock again, imagining what else she might be able to do with her tongue, and the heavy pulse of mounting need at his groin was infuriating. It made him feel out of control and, because he despised that kind of weakness in any part of his life, he gritted his teeth and battled for restraint.

'I've never been the broody sort,' Tabby burbled, licking the fork before dipping it into the delicious dessert again, uncomfortably aware of the dark golden swoop of his gaze following her every move. 'But I was with Sonia when Amber was born and then I had to look after her the first few weeks until Sonia was strong enough after her stroke to leave hospital. I'm afraid that by that stage I was committed heart, soul and body to Amber...our attachment just happened and then Sonia had the second stroke and died immediately.' She paused, clashed with his caramel-shaded eyes and felt her mouth run dry. 'Please stop staring at me.'

'Then stop playing with the fork,' Acheron suggested huskily. 'Naturally I'm picturing you spread across the table as an infinitely more appealing main course than the one I've eaten.'

Surprised colour sprang into her face, and she dropped the fork with a clatter. 'Do you ever think of anything but sex?'

'And you're not thinking about it too?' Acheron derided thickly, studying her with burning intensity.

And the pink in her cheeks burned hotter than ever because he was perfectly correct. His raw masculine virility called to her on a visceral level. The table between them felt like a barrier she wanted to push out of the way. She wanted things she had never wanted before. She wanted to taste that intriguing little triangle of brown male skin visible below his throat, kiss a path along that stubborn jaw line, *touch*, explore. And even worse the mere thought of such experimentation made the blood race through her veins, her nipples tighten and push against her bodice while a liquid sensation of squirming warmth flowered between her thighs. *So, this is lust*, she told herself sharply. *Grow up and deal with it like a woman, not a frightened little girl.*

Acheron thrust back his chair and vaulted to his full commanding height of well over six feet. 'Come on…'

'No, sit down,' Tabby told him shakily, very much afraid that she knew exactly where he wanted her to go and even more afraid that she was ready to say yes, for never in her life had she ever felt anything as powerful as the primitive longing he awakened in her.

'Don't look at me like that and then try to tell me what to do, *hara mou*. It doesn't work,' Acheron advised, strolling round the table to move behind her and tug out the chair with her still seated in it.

'One of us has to try to be sensible,' Tabby protested in desperation.

Acheron bent down and scooped her out of the chair as if she were a child. *'Why?'* he queried thickly, his warm breath fanning her throat. 'We're not hurting anyone. We're both free agents. We can do as we like—'

'That's not how I live.'

'You've trapped yourself in a cage of irrational rules because that makes you feel safe,' Acheron countered, striding across the hall with her still cradled in his arms. 'But I can keep you safe too...'

Only he could still hurt her, just as easily as he could silence her arguments and sweep her literally off her feet, Tabby acknowledged feverishly even as her fingers reached up of their own accord to skate admiringly along the clean, hard line of his jaw. 'You don't make me feel safe.'

'But then you don't trust anyone,' Acheron countered with a swift downward glance at her anxious face. 'Neither do I. Even so, I *can* promise you that I won't lie to you.'

'Not much of a comfort when you could give tips to Machiavelli on how best to get your own way by nefarious means,' Tabby traded, provoking a surprised laugh from Acheron as he mounted the stairs. She knew decision time had come and gone and she wanted his mouth on hers so badly that it literally hurt even to think about it.

He lowered her to the carpet to open the first door, grabbed her hand as though he was afraid she would run off last minute and virtually dragged her into his bedroom. 'Now, I finally have you where I want you. Can you believe that this is our wedding night?'

'But it isn't…we're not really married.' Tabby leant back against his bedroom door, taut with tension because she was sincerely out of her comfort zone and could scarcely breathe for nerves. 'Let's not kid ourselves about that. Neither one of us ever had any plans to make this a proper marriage. I may be wearing a wedding ring but it's meaningless.'

Acheron didn't know a single woman of his acquaintance who would have reminded him of that fact at that precise moment, or who would have come to his bedroom without a carefully set agenda of ambitious and mercenary acquisition in mind. In the strangest possible way, Tabby was a breath of fresh air in his life, he reflected, un-easy with the thought.

'I know.' Like a hunter stalking a wary doe, Acheron approached and closed both of his hands over hers to pull her forward into his arms. 'But nothing that feels as exciting as this could possi-bly be meaningless,' he traded huskily.

'It's only hormones.'

'Says the woman who hasn't a clue what's going to be happening in that bed,' Acheron teased, feathering his mouth hungrily over the soft, silky contours of hers and making her shiver.

'Of course I know what happens…' But she still didn't quite know what she was doing there with him, breaking her rules of self-protection by letting him get that close, risking the vulnerability she always shunned. 'It's just sex,' she told him staunchly.

'It will be amazing sex,' Acheron predicted, skimming the straps down on her dress, pressing his hungry mouth to a slight-boned shoulder while pressing her close, letting her feel the hard-packed urgency in his lean body while reminding himself that he would have to go slow.

'I love your confidence,' Tabby whispered half under her breath.

'I thought it annoyed you.'

Tabby stretched up on tiptoe to link her arms round his neck and tug his handsome dark head down to her level. 'Shut up,' she told him help-lessly, entrapped by dark eyes blazing like a banked golden fire across her face.

Acheron hoisted her off her feet and brought her down at the foot of the bed to flip off her shoes. 'I don't want to hurt you,' he admitted.

'If it hurts, it hurts,' Tabby said prosaically, determined not to surrender to apprehension because, with the single exception of her deep attachment to Amber, she had never felt as much as he made her feel either emotionally or physically. She supposed she was suffering from some kind of idiotic infatuation with him but assumed it would fade as time went on. 'Is this a one-time thing?' she asked him abruptly.

Engaged in slipping off her shoes, Acheron glanced back at her, amusement playing attractively about the wilful, passionate set of his mouth. 'You can't plan everything in advance, Tabby.'

'I do,' she told him tautly. 'I always need to know exactly where I am and what I'm doing.'

And his mouth claimed hers slow and deep and hungry and the tight knot of anxiety inside her unfurled because, in that moment, her senses locked to his, her body screaming with eagerness for more…more…more, and she couldn't stay focused the way she usually did. He unzipped the dress and extracted her from its folds with an ease and exactitude that briefly chilled her because she discovered she couldn't bear to think of him with the other lovers who must have honed his skills.

'What's wrong?' he prompted, more attuned to

her than she had expected, instantly picking up on her renewed tension.

Perhaps she was, at heart, a terribly jealous, possessive person, she reasoned in mortification, troubled by her thoughts and wondering how she could possibly know what she was like when she had never enjoyed a deeper relationship with a man. There she perched, shivering a little in spite of the warmth of the room, suddenly conscious that she was clad only in bra and knickers and that her body was far from perfect.

'Nothing's wrong,' she breathed while he continued to study her troubled face with a frown. *'All right!'* she exclaimed as if he had repeated the question. 'I was just thinking that you're very smooth at stripping clothes off a woman!'

And Acheron burst out laughing, revelling in that honesty, appreciating that she would simply say whatever she thought without considering its impact and instead saying only what he might want to hear. That quality was another rarity in his world. 'Thank you…I think,' he teased.

'And you're still wearing too many clothes,' Tabby protested, all too aware of her own half-naked state as she struggled not to recall that she had really tiny breasts and was pretty skinny everywhere else where it was said to matter to a man. After all, regardless of her deficiencies, he wanted her. That was a certainty that buoyed her up as she watched dark golden eyes flare over her with unashamed desire and appreciation.

He laughed and shed his shirt, kicked off his shoes with the complete unselfconsciousness of a male who had never been inhibited in a woman's presence or constrained by the fear that a woman might not admire what he had to offer. Her throat ran dry as he unveiled the superb expanse of his bronzed torso, exposing the lean, ripped muscles of his six-pack. Poised there, black stubble darkening his handsome jaw, eyes glinting, hair tousled by her fingers with his jeans hanging low on his narrow hips as he unzipped them, he was as gorgeous as a tiger in his prime: glossy and strong and beautifully poised.

She tried and failed to swallow when she saw the tented effect of his boxers, the all too prominent evidence of his readiness outlined by the fine fabric. When his long, elegant hands began to sweep off that final garment she averted her attention and reached back awkwardly to unhook her bra, peeling it off before scrambling below the linen sheet to rip off her knickers in an effort to seem a little more in control than she was.

'I want you *so* much, *koukla mou*,' Acheron growled, yanking the sheet off her from the foot of the bed so that she sat up again, wide-eyed and thunderously aware of her nakedness. 'I also want to see you, *watch* you—'

'There's not a lot to see!' she gasped, her small body crowding back against the banked-up pillows.

Acheron locked a hand round one slender ankle and pulled her very gently down the bed. 'What I see is beautiful,' he breathed thickly, his hungry scrutiny skimming from the tangle of blonde curls at the apex of her thighs to the glorious hint of secret pink beneath and the mouth-watering swell of her breasts topped by prominent pale pink nipples. In one movement he was up on the bed by her side.

'I'm not.'

'Don't want to hear it!' he interrupted, long fingers fisting in the tumble of her golden hair to hold her still as he skated his mouth back and forth over her lips until they parted and his tongue speared inside, delving and exploring with a thoroughness that deprived her of breath and sanity. He could kiss, oh, yes, he could kiss, and then his fingers teased very gently at her straining nipples and he lowered his mouth there, catching a painfully sensitive peak between his lips and plucking it with a tugging intensity that made her nipple throb and arrowed heat straight down into her pelvis.

She trembled, and her spine arched as he pressed her flat on the mattress, dividing his attention now between the distended buds, suckling on her, flicking his tongue back and forth until the tingles of awareness rose like a tide to engulf her. She trembled, insanely aware of the gathering of heat and moisture between her thighs and the intolerable ache building there along with the desperate desire to be touched.

'You're very responsive,' Acheron purred, studying her with heavy-lidded eyes the colour of melted toffee set between the twin fringes of his black lashes. He skimmed a hand down her thigh, stroked her between her legs, and her hips shifted up in supplication. He possessed her swollen mouth again with carnal hunger before he sent a finger delving into her hot, damp heat.

A sound of helpless keening pleasure was wrenched from Tabby. All of a sudden everything she was feeling was centred in that one tormentingly sensitive area of her body. He settled his mouth to her throat and nuzzled a leisurely trail along the side of her neck, awakening nerve endings she had not known she possessed. What she could not understand was that in the space of minutes she had travelled from not being very sure of what she was doing to craving what he was offering with every straining sinew in her body.

'If at any stage you want me to stop, just say so, *koukla mou*,' Acheron husked.

'Wouldn't that be very difficult for you?' she whispered, her hand smoothing down over his muscled chest to discover the thrusting power of his erection.

'I'm not a teenager. I can control myself,' Acheron growled, arching up into her hand as she traced the velvet-smooth hardness of his shaft while marvelling at the size of him. In that field, he had more than she had expected, more width, more length, and she didn't want to think about how on earth he could make them fit as nature had intended. With a slight but perceptible shudder of reaction he relocated her stroking fingers to his muscled abdomen and added, 'As long as you don't do too much of that.'

Satisfied that she could affect him as much as he affected her, Tabby lay back only to release a whimper of startled sound as he circled her clitoris with expert fingers, unerringly striking the exact spot and the exact pace that would drive her over the edge fastest. Her heart was racing when he shifted down the bed, slid between her thighs and employed his mouth there instead. She had known about that, of course she had known, and had never thought she could be that intimate with any man but the insane pleasure he gave her drove all such logic from her mind, and she gasped and writhed and cried out. Enthralled by an exquisite torture of sensation that built and built, her body leapt out of her control altogether and jerked spasmodically into an intense climax that left her weak.

In the aftermath, Acheron rose up over her, lean, dark features taut and flushed with hunger, and she could feel the wide, blunt tip of him at the heart of her, pushing, precisely stretching her inner sheath until a sudden sharp pain made her cry out in surprise, and he froze in place.

'Do you want me to stop?' Acheron prompted raggedly.

'No point now.' Tabby could see he was in no condition to stop, could feel him hard and pulsing and alien inside her. In any case, the pain of his invasion had already faded and the ache of hollow longing he had roused still lingered. She wrapped her arms round him, instinctively urging him on, fingers smoothing across the bronzed satin of his broad back.

'You're so tight,' he rasped, shifting with an athletic lift of his lean hips to surge into her again, deeper, further, harder in a technique that met every physical craving she hadn't known she had. 'I'm incredibly turned on.'

The flood of sensation returned as he withdrew and plunged back into her again, ensuring that she felt every inch of his penetration. The intensity of sensation shocked her and the powerful contracting bands in her pelvis turned her into a fizzing firework of wild excitement. He moved faster and she clung, riding out the electrifying storm of passion with a heart that seemed to be thumping in her eardrums. The explosion of raw pleasure that followed stunned her as the inner convulsions of her body clenched her every muscle tight as a fist. He vented a shuddering groan of completion while the waves of delight went on and on and on, coursing through her thoroughly fulfilled body.

In a dazed state of abstraction, Tabby lay in the tumbled bedding afterwards, watching Acheron stride across the room to retrieve something before vanishing into the bathroom, from which she soon heard the sound of running water. The instant their encounter had finished, the very moment he had attained release, he had rolled away from her and made no effort to touch her again. She was painfully aware of how much she would have liked him to hold her close in a caring, affectionate way that acknowledged their new intimacy and it disturbed her that she should feel so hurt by his withdrawal. After all, she wasn't looking for, or expecting, love or commitment, was she? No, she wasn't that naive.

She had slept with Acheron because for the very first time she had felt a fierce desire to experience that extra dimension with a man. But his swift departure from the bed had disappointed her, leaving her feeling ridiculously used and rejected. That was silly, she told herself firmly, because when it came to what they had just done he had not taken advantage of her in any way. Indeed, to some degree she was willing to acknowledge that *she* had taken advantage of *him* the moment she had estimated that he would undoubtedly possess the erotic skills that were most likely to ensure that she received pleasure from her first experience. That didn't, however, entitle him to forgiveness for disappointing her in the sensitive aftermath of sex.

Slithering out of bed, Tabby swiftly got dressed, finger-combing her tangled hair back off her damp brow before she approached the bathroom door.

A towel linked round his narrow bronzed hips, Acheron was in the act of stepping out of the shower cubicle.

'A-star for the sex, F for failure for the follow-up,' Tabby pronounced with scorn, mentally blocking out the lean, powerful vibrancy of his commanding presence. Yes, Acheron Dimitrakos was gorgeous but in her scheme of things that was unimportant in comparison to the way he treated her.

CHAPTER SEVEN

IN RECEIPT OF that attack, Acheron stiffened in astonishment and angled his arrogant dark head back, his black-as-jet eyes gleaming with angry incomprehension even as his attention lingered on how astonishingly lovely Tabby looked fresh from his bed with her long blonde hair in a waving, tousled mass round her shoulders, her small face warm with self-conscious colour and her ripe pink mouth still swollen from his kisses. Even as he fought to think clearly, his reaction to that view and those thoughts was instantaneous and very physical. 'What the hell are you talking about?'

'The instant you had your satisfaction you leapt out of bed and abandoned me as though I was suffering from some horrid contagious disease,' Tabby condemned. 'Not an experience I would be tempted to repeat—you made me feel like a whore!'

'That's melodramatic nonsense,' Acheron

fielded with derision, willing back his increasing arousal with every fibre of his self-discipline.

'No, I don't think it is. You couldn't even bear to hold me close for thirty seconds,' Tabby reminded him doggedly. 'Well, I think it's sad that the only way you feel comfortable physically touching anyone is in a sexual way.'

Acheron cursed in Greek. 'You don't know me as well as you think you do. But I warned you that I didn't do cuddling.'

'You think that excuses you?' Tabby asked with scornfully unimpressed eyes of violet blue dominating her flushed and furious face. 'It doesn't. It simply shows you up as selfish and inconsiderate, and I deserved better.'

'I don't fake affection for anyone just because it's the acceptable thing to do,' Acheron bit out between clenched teeth. 'And I have so little practice at it, I would feel foolish and uncomfortable!'

And that was the most strikingly truthful thing he had told her about himself to date, Tabby reckoned, stunned by the raw honesty of that irate reply. Indeed his admission of ignorance and discomfiture squeezed her heart like a clenched fist.

Without even thinking about what she was doing, she closed the distance between them, deliberately invading his personal space to stretch her arms round his neck and look up at him.

'Practise on me,' she urged quietly. 'I practised on Amber. I wasn't a very touchy-feely person either before I got to hold her for the first time.'

Acheron swallowed hard, insanely aware that she was making a platonic approach and quite impervious to the reality that below the towel he was still ragingly erect. He didn't want to hug her as though she were his friend; he wanted to shag her senseless. But he knew that option wasn't in the ring at that moment and he closed his arms round her slowly and lifted her to the other side of the big bathroom. 'You shouldn't have got dressed again,' he scolded.

'I assumed we were done,' Tabby confided bluntly.

Acheron bent down and lifted the hem of her dress to take it off over her head. Totally disconcerted, Tabby froze there for a split second, her arms crossed defensively across her bare breasts. 'What are you doing?'

Acheron hooked a finger into her knickers and jerked them down, lifting her again into his arms to trail them off. 'I may have leapt out of bed but I *was* thinking about your comfort,' he breathed as he lowered her down into the warm embrace of the scented water filling the bath. 'Now lie back and relax.'

Thoroughly disconcerted, Tabby surveyed him in wonderment. 'You came in here and ran a bath for me?'

'I hurt you...I thought you'd be sore,' he breathed huskily as he lit the candles in the candelabra by the sink and doused the lights.

'It was just one of those things, not your fault.' But Tabby reddened and sank deeper into the soothingly warm water, resting her head weakly back on the cushioned padding on the rim. In truth she *was* sore, that part of her so tender she was now uncomfortably aware of her pelvic area. What a pair they were, she thought morosely. He couldn't do ordinary affection and she couldn't do sex.

There was a pop as Acheron released a cork

from a champagne bottle and sent bubbling golden liquid down into a pair of goblets.

'Where did that come from? And the candles?' she pressed weakly.

'Honeymoon couple, wedding night? The staff had all the trimmings waiting in the bedroom… It would be a shame not to use them,' Acheron remarked, perching on the side of the bath to offer her a glass of champagne.

'No, thanks. I never drink,' she said stiltedly.

Acheron thrust the glass into her hand. 'Unless you have a drink problem, one glass isn't going to do any damage.'

Her small fingers tensed round the stem. 'No, I don't have a problem but my parents did.'

'That doesn't mean you have to avoid it altogether.'

'I always like to play it safe,' Tabby confided, taking a small sip of the champagne, tiny bubbles bursting below her nose and moistening her skin.

'I'm more of a risk-taker. I enjoy excitement,' Acheron traded wryly.

'I think I could've worked that out for myself.'

Acheron compressed his mouth, his eyes semi-concealed by his black lashes. 'I didn't stay in bed with you because I didn't want you to have unrealistic expectations of our relationship.'

She grasped what he meant immediately and wished she didn't, a tiny pang of hurt pinching somewhere down deep inside her. He didn't want her getting the idea that there was anything more complex between them than straightforward sex. 'I may be inexperienced but I'm not stupid,' Tabby told him with pride.

'And I'm not good with words if I gave you that impression,' Acheron acknowledged grimly. 'Tabby, I don't have conversations like this with women. I've never met a woman like you.'

'Are we *still* talking about me being a virgin?' Tabby asked in a small voice.

'I'm accustomed to women who know the score.'

'I know it too,' Tabby breathed, skimming a glance across his hard-edged profile, her chest tightening with a sense of constraint. 'I'm a very practical person.'

Acheron scanned her small, tight face, the set grip of her tiny hands over her raised knees as he read the valiant defensiveness she used as a screen and his stomach hollowed out at the prospect of hurting her. He had never felt that way around a woman before and he didn't like it at all. She might be fragile but she had made a choice, just as he had done, and they were both adults, he reminded himself impatiently as he straightened again.

At the same moment, Tabby sat up abruptly and set down the champagne flute, water sloshing noisily around her slight body. 'Oh, my goodness, what am I doing in here? I can't stay! The baby monitor is in my bedroom.'

'Melinda will take care of Amber's needs. Relax,' Acheron urged.

'Melinda can't be expected to work twenty-four hours a day. I told her I'd take care of Amber at night,' Tabby countered as she rolled onto her knees, concern for Amber overcoming her self-consciousness, and began to stand up. 'Pass me a towel—'

'No, you stay where you are,' Acheron instructed, his hand closing over her shoulder to press her back into the warm water again. 'I'll collect the monitor and check on Amber as well.'

Her violet eyes widened. '*You*...will?'

Acheron strode back into the bedroom to retrieve his jeans and wandered back to the doorway, dropping the towel with total unself-consciousness to pull on the jeans. 'Why not? You've already shown me what to do with her if she's crying.'

'I wasn't expecting you to help,' Tabby commented. 'It's my job, not yours, after all.'

'Our arrangement isn't that clear cut. This is a joint venture when it comes to me requiring a wife and you requiring an adoptive father figure,' Acheron reminded her, turning on his heel.

Stiff with uncertainty, Tabby lay back in the warm water and sipped the champagne while still feeling thoroughly confused by Acheron's behaviour. She had got him wrong when she condemned him for abandoning her immediately after sex. But then, had the simple act of sex put him into a particularly good mood? Could a man be that basic? In consideration of her needs, he had run her a bath before he went for his shower.

Now he was actually off to check on Amber for her as if the child was something more than the extra baggage she had assumed he deemed her to be. At the same time, however, he had also clearly felt the need to spell out the lowering message that the only thing between him and Tabby was sex. As if she didn't already know that!

Acheron was the ultimate womaniser, steering clear of involvement and commitment. And why shouldn't he? common sense asked. A young, handsome, wealthy male was in high demand in the world of women and had no need to settle on only one. In addition, Acheron had issues but then who didn't after such a childhood as they had both undergone? In remembrance, Tabby suppressed a shiver. He had probably learned just as she had that if you kept everyone at arm's length you didn't get hurt.

But Tabby had moved on from that self-protective stance when she first opened her heart to friendship with Sonia and then Amber and finally understood how much more warm and satisfying life could be with love and loyalty in it. She knew she had lost her business and her first home because she had chosen to personally care for Sonia and Amber but she had no regrets about the choices she had made.

Amber was now her sole responsibility, she recalled, while wondering what she was doing lying back in a luxury bathtub drinking champagne when the baby she loved might be in need of her. In an instant she had clambered dripping out of the bath and swathed herself in a big warm towel, hurriedly patting herself dry before reaching for her dress again. It was time to get back to the real world, she told herself urgently, and there was nothing 'real world' about lounging around lazily in Acheron's opulent bathroom.

Acheron groaned when he heard the baby crying through the monitor. The little plastic speaker was set on the dressing table and as he studied it he became aware that something had been written on the mirror.

'Go home, whore!' someone had printed with what looked like a red felt-tip pen.

Bemused, nerves still jumping at the sound of the baby crying, Acheron hesitated only a moment before striding into the bathroom to snatch up a towel, dampening it and walking back to wipe the mirror clean again before Tabby could see it. For a split second he paused, brooding over the disturbing awareness that only his household staff had access to the bedroom and that one of them clearly wasn't trustworthy. But why leave such a message for Tabby to find? he questioned furiously. She was his wife, his legal wife with every right to be in his house. Who would target Tabby? His handsome mouth down-curved: Kasma was the most likely suspect. Pure rage blazed in Acheron as he dug out his cell phone, called his head of security and brought him up to speed on the development. His temper uneven, he strode off to take care of the baby. She was only a baby, he told himself bracingly, of course he could handle one tiny baby without help.

Amber was sitting upright screaming at the top of her voice, her little face red as fire. Acheron hovered a few feet from the cot. 'Nothing's that bad,' he told Amber in what he hoped was a soothing tone.

Amber lifted up her arms expectantly.

'Do I need to come that close?' Acheron asked

uneasily. 'I'm here. You're safe. I assure you that nothing bad is going to happen to you.'

Amber fixed bewildered brown eyes on him, tears rolling down her crumpled face, and lifted her arms again in open demand.

Acheron released his breath on a slow measured hiss and moved closer. 'I'm no good at the cuddling stuff,' he warned her ruefully, reaching down to lift the child, who startled him by wrapping both arms tightly round his throat and hanging on as firmly to him as a monkey gripping a branch.

An exhausted sob sounded in his ear, and he splayed a big hand across the little girl's back and shifted his fingers in a vague circular motion aimed at soothing her fears. A vague shard of memory featuring a woman's face momentarily froze him where he stood. He didn't recall what age he had been but he had certainly been very small when the woman had come in the night to comfort him, rocking him in her arms and singing to him until he stopped crying. Had that woman been Olympia, Amber's late grandmother and his own mother's former carer? Who else could it have been? Only Olympia had ever shown him concern and treated him as if he was something other than a nuisance part of her well-paid job.

'I owe you,' he told Amber heavily and he re-arranged her awkwardly in his arms and began to rock her, suppressing that rare memory of the past with the profound discomfort that such images always brought him. 'But even for you I can't sing.'

Amber startled him by smiling widely up at him, showing off her two front teeth, and he smiled back before he even knew what he was doing.

And that was how Tabby saw them when she came to a halt in the doorway: Acheron with a tousled black curl falling over his brow, his haunting dark eyes locked to Amber while the most glorious smile lifted his wide, sensual mouth. Barefoot and bare-chested, well-worn jeans hanging low on his lean hips, he looked both extravagantly handsome and unusually human at the same time. Her breath feathered in her throat and her mouth ran dry because that smile was pure sensual dynamite.

'Let me take her,' she proffered quietly. 'I'll put her back in bed.'

'We were managing fine,' Acheron announced, not without pride in the accomplishment as he settled Amber into Tabby's arms. 'Obviously she's not very choosy.'

'Well, you're wrong there. She can actually be quite choosy and can be difficult with some people,' Tabby admitted as she rested Amber down on the changing mat and deftly changed her before placing the child back into her cot, gently stroking her cheek when she grizzled. 'It's bedtime, sweetness. We don't play at bedtime.'

'I'll organise cover for the nights,' Acheron remarked as she joined him in the corridor.

'That's not necessary.'

'You can still go to her if you want but you can't be dragged out of bed *every* night,' he told her drily.

'I'm still the woman who wants to be her mother. It's my duty to be there for her,' Tabby reminded him gently. 'I don't want other people looking after her all the time.'

'Be reasonable.' Acheron paused outside the two doors that led into their separate bedrooms. 'Are you joining me for what remains of the night?'

The ease with which he asked the question disconcerted Tabby because she had assumed that once his lusty curiosity was satisfied she would no longer be of interest to him. His approach both pleased and annoyed her. 'I'm afraid if I did join you, there would have to be rules,' she murmured awkwardly, her hand closing on the handle of her own bedroom door.

'Rules?' Acheron repeated in wonderment. 'Is that your idea of a joke?'

'No, I rarely joke about serious stuff,' Tabby countered gently. 'If you want to hear the rules, ask me.'

'I don't do rules,' Acheron ground out between gritted teeth. 'Perhaps it has escaped your attention, but I'm not a misbehaving child!'

Tabby closed the door quietly in his face.

She had donned one of her slinky new nightdresses before the door opened again. She scrambled hastily below the top sheet and looked across the room enquiringly.

'What bloody rules?' Acheron slung at her, poised hands affixed to his lean hips, his hard-muscled abdomen prominent.

'One,' Tabby enumerated. 'Any relationship we have has to be exclusive and if you plan to stray you have to tell me and finish it decently. No secrets, no sneaking around on me.'

Acheron surveyed her with wild golden eyes of increasingly wrathful incredulity. 'I don't believe I'm hearing this!'

'*Two,*' Tabby continued unconcerned. 'You treat me with respect at all times. If I annoy you, we have it out but not around Amber.'

'You're absolutely out of your mind,' Acheron breathed with unsettling conviction while he studied her with seething, dark golden eyes. 'And I married you.'

'*Three,*' Tabby pronounced woodenly, although her colour was high and her hands clenched into fists by her side. 'I'm not a toy you can pick up and put down again whenever you feel like it. I'm not the entertainment when you're bored. If you treat me well, I will treat you equally well, but if you don't…well, all bets would be off then.'

'Na pas sto dialo!' Acheron murmured wrathfully. 'It means, go to hell, and take your precious rules with you!'

Tabby didn't breathe again until the door had snapped closed behind him and then she lay back in bed, her body feeling heavy as a stone dropped from a height, her tummy rolling like a boat on a storm-tossed sea. Well, that was one way of getting rid of Acheron without losing face, one way of ensuring he was forced to see her as an equal. What else could she have said? Sliding willy-nilly into a casual sexual affair with no boundaries was not her style and with a man as volatile as he was it would be a sure recipe for disaster. But now that the ultimate womanising, free-spirited man knew that she would make major demands, he would be careful to avoid her from now on.

And what sort of idiot was she to feel sad about that fact? She would get over her silly notions about him—of course she would, because there was really no other option open to her. He wanted one thing, she wanted another, so it was better to end it before it got messy and painful and humiliating. Better by far…

In the middle of the night, Acheron went for a cold shower. His erection wouldn't quit and he was still in an unholy rage. Rules, blasted rules. Was he suddenly back at school? Who did she think she was dealing with? Even more crucially, *what* did she think she was dealing with? Did she assume he had got into that bed and somehow signed up for the whole relationship charade? Trust a woman to take a concept as simple as sex and complicate it!

Even so, he was as furious with himself as he was with her. He had suspected that her naivety would lead to problems and he knew he should have listened to his misgivings. But just as the hot blood pulsing through his tense, aching body wouldn't stop, his desire for her had proved unrelenting. He'd had to know what she was like and he'd found out and, even worse, she had been amazing and no sooner had he stopped than he wanted to go again…and again…and again. His even white teeth clenched hard. That fast he was recalling the hot clenching of her tight little body around him, an explicit memory that did nothing to cool his overheated libido.

'So, who's the cutest little baby in the world?' Tabby chattered the next morning while Amber waved her spoon in the air, cheerfully responding to the warm, loving gush of Tabby's appreciation.

Acheron suppressed a groan and slung himself down into a chair by the dining table on the terrace. Baby talk at breakfast time, one more thing she had brought into his life that was not to his taste. First thing in the morning he liked sex and silence and since he had had neither he could not be expected to be in a good mood, he reasoned impatiently. The sight of Tabby in a little red strappy top and shorts that exposed far too much bare creamy skin for his delectation didn't help. Even a glimpse of the tattoo on her arm as she swivelled in her seat failed to switch off the ever-ready pulse at his groin.

Tabby tried to scan Acheron without being obvious about it, sending little flips of her eyes in his direction with her lashes quickly dropping again. He was *so* beautiful; it was surely a sin for a male to be so beautiful that she was challenged to stop staring at him. Even the awareness of the lingering tenderness between her legs couldn't dull her appreciation of that long, lean, powerful frame of his, gracefully draped in the chair like a work of art to be admired. The sunlight glittered over his black springy curls, and she wanted to run her fingers through his hair, stroke that stubborn jaw line set like granite until she awakened that wonderful smile again. Disconcerted by her treacherous thoughts, Tabby twisted her head away, resisting temptation.

Amber extended both arms in Acheron's direction and beamed at him. 'Not right now, *koukla mou*,' he murmured. 'Have your breakfast first.'

That he had acknowledged Amber's presence but not hers aggravated Tabby. Last night she had only been a body but this morning she was evidently invisible into the bargain. 'Good morning, Acheron,' she said curtly.

'Kalimera, yineka mou,' Ash murmured silkily, noting the fiery brightness of her extraordinary

violet eyes as she settled her gaze on him. 'Did you sleep well?'

'Like a log,' Tabby lied, wondering why he brought out a mean streak in her that she had never known she had.

A maid poured his coffee, and the rich aroma flared her nostrils, inexplicably reminding her that Sonia had become preternaturally sensitive to certain smells when she first fell pregnant with Amber and an edge of panic suddenly sliced through Tabby's surface calm. 'Last night...' she prompted abruptly, waiting with a rapidly beating heart and hot cheeks for the maid to retreat. 'You *did* use protection, didn't you?'

Magnificently nonchalant in the face of that intimate question, Acheron widened lustrous, dark golden eyes in mocking amusement. 'You think I would be stupid enough to neglect such a precaution?'

'I think in the heat of the moment if you wanted something enough you would take risks,' Tabby admitted tautly.

Acheron lifted a winged ebony brow and cocked his handsome head in Amber's direction. 'Not if it meant risking the acquisition of one of those,' he declared. 'Passion doesn't rule me.'

'Or me,' she echoed half under her breath. As she leant forward to help Amber clear her plate, her breasts stirred beneath her tee with the movement, pushing her unbearably sensitive nipples against the fabric, and made her think that a bra would have been a better idea than going without. Particularly in Acheron's radius.

The same view was not wasted on Acheron either, who recalled the precise pout of her delicate flesh and his almost overpowering desire to eat her alive. While the smouldering silence at the table stretched, the nanny entered and removed Amber from her chair to bear her off for a bath.

Acheron dragged in a deep, cooling breath of the sunshine laden air, knowing that, for the sake of peace and better understanding, he had to challenge Tabby's misconceptions. 'Your rules?' he mused with a dismissive shrug of one broad shoulder. '*My* rules? I never ever get involved with clingy, needy women.'

Coming at her out of nowhere, that statement crashed down on Tabby like a brick dropped on glass and her head flew up, violet eyes wide. 'Are you calling me clingy and needy?'

'What do you think?'

Tabby sprang out of her chair, the feet of it slamming back noisily across the tiles underfoot as she stabbed her hands down on the table for support. Anger had gripped her in a stormy surge. 'How dare you? I've never been clingy or needy in my life with a man!'

'Yet your first move is to try and hedge me round with rules. You want reassurance and promises about a future that is unknown to both of us,' Acheron reasoned with cold precision. 'I don't own a crystal ball.'

'I don't like the way you operate!' Tabby vented fiercely.

'Yet you know nothing about me. For years I've been exclusive in my affairs and I don't move on without saying so when I lose interest,' Acheron declared lazily, rising upright to study her, his brilliant, dark eyes hard and glittering. 'It is offensive that you should condemn me for lies and infidelity on the basis of your assumptions about my character.'

'You're so smooth…I wouldn't trust a word that came out of your mouth!' Tabby hurled at him accusingly, refusing to acknowledge that he had a point.

'Now who's guilty of prejudice?' Acheron riposted with soft sibilance. 'What do you find most offensive about me? My public-school education, my wealth or my lifestyle?'

Ferocious resentment held Tabby rigid where she stood, her small face taut and flushed with indignation, but it was the soft pink fullness of her lush mouth that welded Acheron's attention there. 'What I find most offensive is your certainty that you know best about *everything*!'

'I do know that we are poles apart and that this arrangement will work most efficiently if we stick to the original agreement we made.'

Tabby's tummy flipped as though she had gone down in a lift too fast, sheer strain locking her every muscle into tautness. 'You should've kept your blasted hands off me!' she slammed back.

Acheron flashed her a grim appraisal from his stunning golden eyes, and his mouth twisted sardonically. 'Sadly, I *couldn't*…'

And with that final admission, Acheron strode back into the air-conditioned cool of the villa and left her alone to contemplate the truly fabulous view. The rolling green Tuscan hills stretched out before her marked out in a colourful patch-work of woodland, olive groves and vineyards. She snatched in a deeply shaken breath, the hot air scouring her lungs. He wanted them to re-turn to the sensible terms of their platonic agree-ment, which was exactly what she had believed she wanted. Why, then, when she had achieved her goal, did she feel as though she had lost the battle? Indeed, instead of feeling relieved and re-assured by his logical approach to their differ-ences, she felt ridiculously hurt and abandoned…

CHAPTER EIGHT

TABBY ROLLED THE soft ball back to Amber where the child sat below the dappled shade of an ancient spreading oak tree. Amber rolled over and crawled to the edge of the rug, a look of glee in her bright eyes as she scanned the wide green expanse of freedom open before her.

Tabby marvelled at the speed with which the little girl had learned to embrace independent movement. One minute she had been rolling over and over again to explore further afield and the next she had perfected crawling. At just over seven months old she was a fairly early developer but she had always been a physically strong baby who met every developmental guideline in advance, and Tabby wasn't really surprised that Amber had discovered how to get around without adult assistance ahead of time. As she watched the little girl pulled a blade of grass and stuck it in her mouth.

'No…no,' she was saying while retrieving the grass when Melinda strolled up and offered to give her a break.

'Yes, and you're welcome,' Tabby confided ruefully. 'She's much more of a handful now, and I wouldn't mind a little break to sunbathe and read.'

'We can manage that. I'm going to put her in the buggy and take her for a walk,' the blonde nanny told her smoothly. 'I just love it here.'

Tabby glanced at the younger woman, wondering why she found it such a challenge to like her and feeling rather guilty about the fact. After all, Melinda was great with Amber, a diligent worker and friendly. Perhaps it was the hungry little glances she often saw Melinda aiming at Acheron that had prevented Tabby from bonding more with the other young woman. It was not that she was jealous, Tabby reasoned uneasily, simply that she wasn't comfortable with a woman prepared to show that much interest in the married man who employed her. In any case, and to be fair to all parties concerned, Acheron had shown not the smallest awareness of Melinda's curvaceous blonde allure.

'Any idea when we'll be leaving here yet?' Melinda asked as she gathered up Amber's toys and stuffed them in a bag.

'Not yet, sorry…my husband hasn't decided how long we'll be staying,' Tabby replied, wryly impressed by the way that possessive label slid off her tongue. But that, she had learned, was the easiest way to refer to Acheron in front of the staff.

Yet he was as much a husband as a caged tiger in a zoo would be, she conceded unhappily, lifting her book and her sunglasses and heading for the cool courtyard in which the pool was situated. For the past week she had barely seen Acheron, who confined himself to his office most of the day and often half the night to work. Even when he was around his phone was always ringing and his single-minded focus on business was exactly what she should have expected from a goal-orientated alpha male.

Occasionally he would join her for a cup of coffee at breakfast time and he generally put in a rather silent appearance at the dinner table, eating quickly and then politely excusing himself. He was a cool and distant companion at those meals and there was never so much as a hint of sexual awareness in either his looks or his conversation. It was as though that wild bout of passion on their wedding night was the product of her imagination alone, but Tabby still found it a distinct challenge to revert to treating him like a stranger and that embarrassed her, denting her pride and her belief in her own strength and independence because no woman of character should continue to crave the attention of a man set on treating her like the wallpaper.

Yet amazingly, infuriatingly, Acheron was playing an entirely different ball game with Amber. Melinda swore that Acheron never passed the nursery door without coming in to talk to and play with her charge and Amber had already learned to make a beeline for Acheron whenever he was in her vicinity. In fact, when it came to Acheron, Amber took her welcome for granted. Maybe Acheron's ego was flattered by the amount of attention Amber gave him. Maybe he was even belatedly discovering that he actually liked and enjoyed the company of children? How could she possibly know what motivated his interest? Tabby had not got through a week of virtually sleepless nights without acknowledging that she knew very little at all about Acheron Dimitrakos. Her husband was a mystery to her in almost every conceivable way.

Acheron stood at the window and groaned at the sight of Tabby arranging her slim pale body on a lounger like an exhibition banquet for the starving. A purple bikini cupped her rounded little breasts and slender hips and every shift of her slim thighs drew his considerable attention. He shifted uneasily, struggling to rein back the heavy pulse of arousal that was making his nights so long and frustrating.

Although he had kept watch, as he told himself a protective husband should do, he had yet to see Tabby go topless to eradicate the risk of tan marks. He frowned, not wanting her to show that amount of naked flesh when there were always staff roaming the grounds. It was very strange, he acknowledged in bewilderment, that in spite of the fact he thought it was a very old-fashioned attitude, which he would not have admitted even under torture, he didn't like the idea of anyone but him seeing any part of Tabby bare. He thought that there was a very weird possessive streak in him somewhere and blamed it on the surprising fact that he had become his wife's first lover.

His wife, a label he had never thought he would use, he conceded hard-mouthed, his dark eyes hooded and unusually reflective. Had Tabby genuinely been his wife, however, she would have been in his bed throughout the long hot hours of the afternoon abandoning herself to the demands of his passion and losing herself in the release he would have given her. As his body hardened afresh under the onslaught of that X-rated imagery he cursed bitterly under his breath.

Regretfully, Tabby had all the flexibility of a steel girder: he could do the rules or he could do cold showers. There would be no halfway measures, no get-out clause with her. It would be all or nothing and he knew he *couldn't* do it, couldn't walk that line and change himself to suit when he knew there was no future in it. It wouldn't be fair to her. Yet right at that precise moment Tabby's rules had more pulling power than a ten-ton truck.

* * *

That evening, Tabby selected a drop-dead gorgeous blue dress from the closet. Over the past week she had worn a different outfit every day, reasoning that the clothes were there and there was little point wasting them. In any case it would be downright silly to choose to overheat in the jeans and tops that were virtually all she had left of her own clothes since her life first began to unravel after she had lost her own home. Back then she had had to surrender an awful lot of her possessions, whittling her collection of clothing and objects down until she retained only what mattered most and what she could carry.

She tossed the dress on the bed, put on her make-up and brushed her hair, not that how she looked mattered when Acheron was treating her as though she were someone's maiden aunt. But then Acheron *wasn't* the reason why she took the trouble to dress up, she reminded herself staunchly. She did it for her own self-esteem and the knowledge that behaving, at least on the outside, like a rich honeymoon bride was part of her role. Clothed, she eased her feet into perilously high heels and surveyed herself critically in the mirror, mouth momentarily drooping while she wished she were taller, curvier and more striking in appearance…like Kasma? The Kasma whom Acheron never, ever mentioned? But then what business was Kasma of hers? The fiery fury, ignited only a week before by the discovery that Acheron would benefit as much as she did from their marriage, had drained away. After all, she had married Acheron for only one reason: to become Amber's adoptive mother, and all she needed to focus on now was getting through their little charade of a marriage as smoothly and painlessly as possible. Worrying about anything else, *wanting* anything else was unnecessarily stressful and stupid.

Acheron was crossing the hall when Tabby reached the head of the marble staircase. Obeying instinct, she threw her head back and straightened her spine even as she felt perspiration break out across her skin. There he was, sleek, outrageously good-looking and sophisticated even when clad in jeans and an open-necked shirt. Her heart went bumpety-bumpety-bump like a clock wound up too tight, and she gripped the bannister with an agitated hand to start down the stairs. Unfortunately for her, her leading foot went down, however, not onto a step but disorientatingly into mid-air and she tipped forward with a shocked cry of fright, her hand slipping its light hold on the stair rail, her whole body twisting as she tried to halt her fall so that her hip struck the edge of a hard marble step and her ankle was turned beneath her.

'I've got you!' Acheron bit out as the world steadied again.

Mercifully Tabby registered that she was no longer falling but that pain was biting all the way from her hip down her leg…no, not her leg, her ankle. She adjusted as Acheron swept her up into his arms with too much enthusiasm and her leg swung none too gently and she couldn't bite back the cry of pain that was wrenched from her throat. 'My ankle…'

'*Thee mou*…you could've been killed falling on these stairs!' Acheron breathed with a rawness that took her aback, striding back down into the hall with his arms tautly linked round her slight body. He called out in Greek until one of his security staff came running and then he rapped out instructions.

Against her cheek she could feel the still-accelerated pounding of his heart and she wasn't surprised that he was still high on adrenalin because he must have moved faster than the speed of light to intercept her fall. She felt quite queasy at the realisation that but for his timely intervention she might have fallen all the way down the marble staircase and broken her neck or at the very least a limb or two. Relief that she had only wrenched her ankle and bruised herself filtered slowly through her. 'I'm OK… Lucky you caught me in time.'

Acheron laid her down with exaggerated care on a sofa and squatted athletically down to her level. 'Did you feel anyone push you?' he asked, brilliant dark heavily fringed eyes locked to her face.

She was astounded at the tenor of that question; her violet eyes rounded. 'Why would anyone push me down the stairs?' she asked weakly. 'I lost my balance and tripped.'

Acheron frowned. 'Are you certain? I thought I saw someone pass by you on the landing just before you fell.'

'I didn't see or hear anyone.' Her brows pleated and her lashes screened her eyes, the heat of embarrassment washing away her pallor because she knew exactly *why* she had tripped but wild horses wouldn't have dragged the confession from her. 'Yes, of course I'm certain.'

If she hadn't been so busy admiring Acheron and trying to pose like a silly teenager to look her very best for his benefit, she would never have missed her step, Tabby was reflecting in deep, squirming chagrin.

'I'm afraid I have to move you again…I'll try not to hurt you,' Acheron told her, sliding his hands beneath her prone length. 'But I have to get you into a car to get you to a doctor.'

'For goodness' sake, I don't need a doctor!' Tabby exclaimed in growing embarrassment.

But over the next couple of hours while she was subjected to every possible medical examination at the nearest hospital, she might as well have been talking to a wall because Acheron refused to listen to a word she said. Furthermore, far from behaving like the cool, reserved male she was accustomed to dealing with, Acheron was clearly all wound up although why he was, she had no idea. He paced the floor outside her examination cubicle, talked to her through the curtain to check she was all right and not in too much discomfort, insisted on an X-ray being done while virtually ignoring the doctor who assured him that she was suffering from nothing more serious than some nasty bruising and a sprained ankle. Even more embarrassing, his security team spread out round them on full systems alert as if awaiting an imminent rocket attack on the casualty department.

'Ah...very much the adoring and anxious husband,' the middle-aged doctor chuckled in his ignorance.

If only the man knew how wrong he was, Tabby thought unhappily, feeling like a wretched nuisance and a malingerer taking up valuable medical attention when really there was nothing very much amiss with her.

If Tabby had died, it would have been *his* fault. Acheron brooded on that thought darkly, rage and guilt slivering through him in sickening waves and like nothing he had ever felt before. But then he had never been responsible for another life before and, though he would have liked to have thought otherwise, he believed that his wife was very much *his* responsibility. Naturally he was appalled by the suspicion that someone who worked for him might have attempted to hurt his wife. Having seen the rude message left on her bedroom mirror, he was unimpressed by her conviction that she had simply had an accident. In the split second it had taken for Tabby to lose her balance and topple she might not even have noticed that someone had lightly pushed her or tripped her up.

He was even more frustrated that his security staff had failed to come up with anything suspicious on any member of the villa staff. Acheron's mouth twisted. Unfortunately the Tuscan villa had rarely been used, hence the renovation the previous year and the hire of employees who were a new and unknown quantity and whose dependability would only be confirmed by the test of time. His lustrous eyes hardened and his stubborn mouth compressed into a tough line of determination. Tabby's safety was paramount and as he was very reluctant to frighten her with his suspicions. The wisest strategy would be to immediately vacate the villa and seek a more secure setting. That decision reached, Acheron gave the order, refusing to back down even when the chief of his security pointed out that such a move would entail rousing the baby from her bed as well. Regardless of the drawbacks of his plan, Acheron could hardly wait to get Tabby and the baby away from the Tuscan villa, which now, to his way of thinking, seemed a tainted place. He watched the doctor bandaging her swollen ankle, annoyance still gripping him that he had failed to prevent her from getting hurt.

'Sorry about all this.' Tabby sighed in the limo as they left the hospital.

'When you have an accident you don't need to apologise for it. How are you?' Acheron pressed.

'A bit battered and sore—nothing I won't quickly recover from,' Tabby responded with a smile. 'It'll certainly teach me to be more careful on stairs from now on.'

Acheron was quietly stunned. No woman of his acquaintance would have neglected to make a huge fuss over such an incident by exaggerating their injuries and demanding his sympathy and attention. Tabby, however, characteristically downplayed the episode and asked nothing of him, an acknowledgement that only increased his brooding discomfiture with the situation.

'Where on earth are we going?' Tabby enquired as he lifted her out of the limo and stowed her in the wheelchair already waiting for her use. 'Is this the airport?'

'Yes, we're flying to Sardinia,' Acheron said casually.

'Seriously? I mean, like *right now*?' Tabby stressed in disbelief. 'It's ten o'clock at night.'

'Amber and her nanny are already on board the helicopter, as is your luggage,' Acheron admitted.

There were many things Tabby could have said but she was fighting a dropped jaw and had already learned to think twice before she spoke her mind around Acheron. She clamped her lips firmly together and assumed that he was bored at the villa and that the evident appeal of a change of surroundings had persuaded him to act on impulse. Not only was he dragging Amber out of bed, but he was also forcing Tabby to travel when she was exhausted and in pain. Her lush mouth down-curved: he was being selfishly inconsiderate but she supposed that was normal behaviour for a male accustomed to thinking only of his own needs.

The helicopter was very noisy and Tabby, who hadn't eaten since lunchtime, was almost sick with hunger. She insisted on taking Amber from Melinda, though, and soothed the overtired baby herself. She was surprised when Acheron eased the drowsing child from her arms and settled her on his lap instead. Amber looked up at him, stuck her thumb back in her mouth and closed her eyes again, seemingly content with the exchange. Tabby must've dozed off at that point because she wakened confused by the bright light on her face and the jabs of pain from her ankle as Acheron carried her into a house.

'How do you feel?' he enquired again, stunning gaze sweeping her pale, taut face.

'I'll be fine—'

'Don't be a martyr—you look like death warmed over,' he countered impatiently. 'You're going straight to bed, *yineka mou*. I've organised food as well.'

A bed and a meal sounded very appealing to Tabby at that moment. He mounted a staircase and a faint breeze cooled her cheekbone. Her lashes swept up on a tall open window framed by pale fluttering draperies just as Acheron laid her down on a ginormous bed and began to carefully ease the bedding from beneath her. It struck her that for once he was being very kind and that set her teeth on edge.

'Why are you being so nice to me all of a sudden?' Tabby demanded abruptly.

That single question said so much that Acheron didn't want to hear just then that he almost groaned his frustration aloud. Leave it to Tabby, he thought ruefully. Leave it to Tabby to say what nobody else dared to say to Acheron Dimitrakos. He breathed in slowly. 'You're hurt.'

'You don't do rules and I don't do pity,' Tabby told him, tilting her chin in challenge.

'You're my wife.'

'Not really.'

'*Enough* my wife that I want to treat you like one,' Acheron contradicted almost harshly.

Tabby screened eyes blank with incomprehension and she was horribly tempted by an urge to slap him. He should have come with a dictionary or some sort of instruction manual that explained how he worked because once again she was all at sea as to what went on his complex and infuriating head.

'I want to make you feel better,' Acheron announced.

'No pity parties here, please.'

'I haven't behaved very well,' Acheron muttered in a harsh driven undertone. 'I am trying to make amends.'

'Pity's pity,' Tabby told him, unmoved by that argument.

Acheron came down on the bed beside her. There was something wild about the glitter in his seething golden eyes as he gently knotted one hand in the fall of her golden hair and closed his mouth hungrily over hers. He sent a jolt of such savage hunger rocketing through her that she froze in sheer fright.

'Does that feel like pity?' he growled.

Tabby made no comment because she could barely breathe. She wanted him to do it again and for longer and was only just able to keep her hands off that lean, powerful body so very close to hers for the first time in a week. One little touch and he made her feel like a sex addict ready to run scarily out of control. In sudden retreat, she dropped her head and then mercifully they were interrupted by the entrance of a woman carrying a tray.

'You need to eat,' Acheron told her unnecessarily.

With his assistance, Tabby leant back against the pillows and lifted the knife and fork. She literally didn't *dare* look at him again, couldn't trust herself that far, knew that she couldn't risk reliving that burning, driving sensation of sexual need in his presence. Hungry though she undoubtedly was, she had to force herself to eat because the sheer level of tension holding her taut was suppressing her appetite. She ate in silence while

Acheron paced restively round the big room, constantly drawing her eyes until she remembered that she couldn't afford to look, and in fact had to blank him out to stay in control. And what did that say about her? Was she really that weak that she couldn't withstand him? This guy who had virtually ignored her for the past week? The same one who had slept with her and then backed off at supersonic speed? Shame engulfed her, increasing the exhaustion she had been fighting to contain.

The tray was removed from her lap. Her lashes drooped, eyes so heavy she literally couldn't hold them open any longer.

'Get some sleep,' Acheron urged, and for once she was in the mood to obey.

Tabby awoke with a piercing need to go to the bathroom, eyes flickering open on darkness and a strong feeling of disorientation. She struggled to sit up and gasped in dismay at the pain that shot through her ankle while she stretched out a wildly flailing hand in search of a bedside light. Mercifully she found the switch attached to a hanging wire, and light illuminated the bedroom a scant second before the male lying on a sofa against the wall leapt upright.

'Ash?' she whispered in disbelief. 'What are you doing in here?'

Acheron was bare-chested and barefoot, low-slung denim jeans clinging to his lean hips. Her startled gaze clung to the muscled expanse of his magnificent bronzed torso and then flicked guiltily higher to take in the dark stubble masking his lower jaw and the unnerving intensity of eyes that glittered like black diamonds in the low light. 'I couldn't leave you in here alone.'

'Why not?' Tabby queried, her face hotter than fire as she forced herself to swivel her hips and shift her good leg off the edge of the bed. 'Why would you sleep on a sofa for my benefit?'

'What on earth are you trying to do?' Acheron demanded, striding across the room.

'I need the bathroom,' she breathed between gritted teeth, mortification rolling over her like a tidal wave.

'You are so stubborn, *koukla mou*. Right now, you need help and I didn't want to put a stranger in here with you,' he admitted impatiently, pushing the walking stick resting against the bedside cabinet into her hand and then slowly pulling her upright to take advantage of its support. 'Now go slow or you'll hurt yourself.'

But Tabby had already worked out that there was no way of moving her leg without her ankle hurting her and she simply clenched her teeth and got on with it, tears stinging her eyes as she hobbled clumsily towards the connecting door he had already opened for her benefit.

Acheron groaned something in Greek and carefully scooped her up into his arms to carry her into the bathroom and gently settle her down on the stool by the vanity unit. 'Pain's always worse in the middle of the night. You'll feel better tomorrow,' he predicted. 'Shout when you're ready to go back to bed.'

Reckoning that there would be two blue moons in the sky before she willingly asked for his help, Tabby studied her tousled reflection in the mirror in cringing horror. She was still wearing the make-up she had put on for dinner the night before and she had panda eyes, sleep creases on her cheek and hideously messy hair. How come he looked gorgeous in the middle of the night but she looked like the Bride of Dracula?

She glanced down and fingered the skimpy nightdress she now wore and swallowed back a groan. Acheron must've undressed her. So what? He had already seen her naked, she reminded herself doggedly, so he had seen nothing new and it was very silly to be embarrassed about it. Levering herself upright, she took care of necessities and then made use of the facilities to clean herself up as best she could. Feeling considerably fresher but pale and stiff with the amount of pain her every movement had made her suffer, Tabby hobbled back out of the bathroom.

Acheron was waiting to scoop her up and deposit her back on the bed.

'I still don't understand what you're doing here with me,' she said weakly, perspiration breaking out on her brow.

'There're only three bedrooms in the main house. I knew you wouldn't want Amber staying away from you in the staff quarters and Melinda needed the third room,' Acheron explained drily.

'There's *only* three bedrooms?' Tabby remarked in amazement. 'You really didn't plan this move very well, did you?'

Acheron dealt her a fulminating appraisal in seething silence. 'It's three in the morning…let's talk about it tomorrow.'

Tabby watched him move back towards the sofa and released her breath on a reluctant sigh. 'Oh, for goodness' sake, share the bed… It's as big as a football pitch. I'm sure we can manage to avoid each other.'

Acheron swung round, his surprise unfeigned, but he said nothing. He switched out the light, and she lay very still in the darkness, listening to the sound of his jeans coming off and trying very hard not to picture what he looked like without them. The sheet moved, the mattress depressed and she forced herself to relax. She was safe as houses with him, she told herself wryly. Acheron was powered by reason, not emotion, not passion. He knew they were a match made in hell.

It was dawn by the time Tabby woke again. Soreness and stiffness assailed her with her first involuntary movement, and she screwed up her face in silent complaint. She turned her head only for her breath to hitch at the sight of Acheron lying asleep only inches away from her. His hair, rumpled into ebony curls, stood out in stark contrast to the white pillow case, his black lashes luxuriant fans that rimmed his strong cheekbones, his wilful passionate mouth full and relaxed. She couldn't stop staring at him. The sheet was wrapped round his hips, the corrugated musculature of his bronzed chest and abdomen exposed as well as a long, powerful, hair-roughened thigh. The pure haunting beauty of his perfectly sculpted body grabbed her by the throat and shook her inside out while heat pooled in her pelvis. She wanted to touch him; she wanted to touch him so badly it hurt to be denied.

His lashes swept up and he stretched slowly and languorously, long, taut muscles defined like ropes below his smooth brown skin. *'Kalimera, yineka mou.'*

Tabby arched a brow. 'Which *means*…?'

'Good morning, wife of mine,' Acheron translated with rich amusement lightening his dark eyes.

'I'm not yours,' Tabby hissed back faster than a striking rattler.

A lean brown hand lifted and wound slowly and carefully into the tumbled fall of her blonde hair, his glittering dark golden eyes hot as boiling honey on her skin. 'How else would you describe yourself? You married me and then you accepted my body into yours. Don't you appreciate that that means that we legally consummated our union?'

Seized by chagrin and confusion, Tabby stiffened. 'I...I...'

He covered her mouth with his, lingering to nibble teasingly at her full lower lip before moving on to taste her with explosive eroticism. A chemical reaction took place inside her, her body jerking in response while within seconds a giant mushroom of heated hunger and longing surged up inside her, blowing her best intentions to hell. Helpless in the grip of that sensual offensive, she kissed him back and his tongue drove deep between her lips with a raw sexual charge that roared through her like a rocket attack.

'Ash?' she mumbled when he freed her long enough to breathe again.

He stared down at her with lancing impatience, every line of him rigid with tension. 'To hell with your rules,' he growled in a tone of decision, his broad chest vibrating against her swollen breasts. 'I only play by my own.'

Those words were still ringing in her ears when he slid his hands underneath her and lifted her slowly onto her side. 'What are you doing?' she gasped.

'I'm making what we both need possible,' Acheron rasped in her ear, his warm breath fanning her neck as he buried his mouth in the sensitive slope between neck and shoulder while his hands slid up from her waist to cup her achingly tender breasts. 'As you're in no condition to run away, shout loud if you want to say no.'

In stark disconcertion her violet eyes opened to their fullest extent and locked onto the sofa he had occupied the night before. She had invited him into the bed in the first place. Had he assumed her body was included in the offer? Or was he just as entrapped as she was by the chemistry between them? Naturally that latter interpretation pleased her more but, in the midst of her pondering, long fingers plucked at the straining peaks of her breasts and actual thought became too much of a challenge.

Acheron tasted the soft white skin of her throat and the sweet scent of her enclosed him, heightening his arousal to an almost unbearable extent. In need of release he pressed his throbbing erection against her bottom, and she gasped and leant back into him while he lifted her nightdress to caress the swollen bounty of her small, taut breasts, paying special attention to her plump pink nipples. 'I love your breasts,' he told her thickly. 'They fit perfectly into my hands, *moli mou.*'

Every tiny muscle straining as she trembled, Tabby looked down at the fingers, so dark against her paler skin, expertly caressing her. Sharp biting arrows of need were spearing down between her legs where her indescribably sensitive flesh was tingling. She shifted and a faint sound of discomfort was wrenched from her as she accidentally moved her ankle.

'Lie still,' Acheron urged. 'You don't need to do anything. Let me do all the work.'

Her desire was already so strong that she wanted to scream, wanted to tell him what to do and to do it quickly. The shock of the thought and a vision of his reaction cooled her teeming thoughts. But she hadn't known, hadn't ever dreamt that a kiss and a little intimate touching could send her temperature shooting from zero to overload and she knew that she was finally understanding the very basic reason why he had become her first lover. He burned her up like a lightning strike, awakened a craving that overwhelmed her defences.

His hand shimmied down over her thigh, flirting, teasing more intimate areas without delivering on the promise. She ached, she actually ached deep down inside where she felt hollow and desperate, her entire being locked to the playful passage of that provocative hand. Fingertips traced her hidden core, stroking nerve endings that were impossibly delicate. She dragged in a sustaining breath while he nibbled an enervating path down the side of her extended throat. 'In a minute I'm going to kill you,' she swore shakily.

'No, you're going to ask me to do it again.'

'You really don't suffer from low self-esteem,' she noted even more unevenly, her breath catching in her convulsing throat as a fingertip brushed her clitoris, and flame leapt through her entire core.

'Not between the sheets…no,' Acheron agreed silkily.

'You've been told you're wonderful?'

'Many times. I'm filthy rich. Telling me I'm rubbish in bed—even if it's true—wouldn't be profitable,' he advanced with cynical cool.

Consternation seized Tabby. 'That's *awful*—'

'Awful,' he mimicked, stroking the most sensitive spot on her whole body so that she jackknifed back against him with a startled yelp.

'I don't want your money,' Tabby exclaimed helplessly. 'I just want your body!'

A stark little silence fell, and she squeezed her eyes tight shut in horror. *I didn't say that, I couldn't possibly have said that!*

'I've got no objections to that goal,' Acheron husked, biting at her ear lobe with erotic intent, ostensibly undeterred by her claim. 'It's earthy and honest…why not?'

He touched her again and her mortification drowned in a sea of shivering response. She lay back against him, tiny muscles twitching, soothed by the heat and strength of him even as that amplified physical contact heightened her awareness. With immense delicacy he stroked the seam of her femininity and then slid inside where she was warm and wet and, oh, so needy. She quivered, pitched straight to a high of longing that she couldn't quell or even control. He sank a finger inside her, and she jerked and gasped as he plunged slowly in and out, raising her temperature to boiling point, making her squirm and shift, forgetting even the twinges of pain in her ankle.

'Hot, tight, ready,' Acheron growled hungrily in her ear as she arched back into his lean, hard body, instinctively seeking the fulfilment that only he could give while he angled away from her to don a condom. 'I've been fantasising about this for days.'

'*Days?*' she parroted in surprise as he lifted her undamaged leg to spread her open for him.

'Every night since that first night, every day I saw you in that teeny tiny bikini, *glyka mou,*' Acheron confided, tilting her forward, long fingers tightening their hold on her slender thigh as he entered her with a groan of intense masculine satisfaction.

A muffled scream of pleasure was torn from Tabby's throat as her body was forced to adjust to his size, her inner channel stretching to the brink of insane pleasure.

'All right?' Acheron murmured thickly.

'Well, I wouldn't want you to answer your phone right now!' Tabby admitted shakily, her heart thundering, her blood racing, her whole body thrumming with sensation as he eased back and then slammed into her again, jolting her with wicked pleasure.

'No boundaries!' he ground out forcefully. 'No boundaries between us!'

She couldn't think, couldn't speak for the intensity of what he was making her feel. He tugged her head back and took her mouth with passionate, driving need and the taste and heat of him scorched her all the while the slow, sure thrust of his engorged shaft stimulated her senses to an unbearable peak of excitement. Her hips writhed. The pace quickened. The heat built. She was crying out, sobbing she knew not what when her wayward body finally clamped down convulsively on him and she soared over the edge in a frenzied crescendo of release that took her by storm.

Ecstasy was still rippling through her weak body in small blissful waves when he wrapped his arms round her and kept her close.

'You're amazing,' he husked.

'You too,' she whispered, exhaustion pinning her to the bed.

'And we're going to do this over and over again,' Acheron decreed with lethally sexy assurance. 'No more cold showers, no more separate beds, no more posing in teeny tiny bikinis I can't rip off.'

'Sleepy,' she framed apologetically.

'Sleep...you're going to need all your energy,' he said.

CHAPTER NINE

WHEN TABBY WOKE for the fourth time in twelve hours, she was totally disorientated and she blinked in the strong sunlight flooding through the French windows. A split second later, she sat up and checked her watch to discover that it was mid-afternoon.

My goodness, she had slept half the day away! In guilty dismay, she clambered awkwardly out of bed, learning that Acheron had got it right when he had suggested she would feel better in the morning. Her hip still ached like the very devil but the pain in her ankle had become more bearable. Curious to see her surroundings, having arrived in complete darkness the night before, she limped over to the French windows with the aid of her stick and went out onto the sunlit balcony to stand at the rail.

A craggy cove stretched out below her, the towering rocks encircling a stretch of pure white sand lapped by a turquoise sea so clear she could see the ocean bottom. The lush tree-filled gardens ran right to the edge of the beach. It was absolutely idyllic and very beautiful but Tabby's attention was drawn straight to the couple standing together in the rippling surf. Amber's pram was parked in the shadow of the rocks and Melinda, clad in a minuscule red bikini that exaggerated her bountiful curves, was talking with apparent urgency to Acheron, whose lean, powerful body was sheathed only in trunks.

It was an unexpectedly intimate and disturbing sight, and Tabby couldn't take her eyes off the couple, jealousy spearing through her with an immediacy that appalled her. She jerked in dismay and snatched in a startled breath when Melinda rested a hand down on Acheron's arm. To his credit the contact only lasted for a second because he took an immediate step back from the forward blonde and with a brief final word strode back across the sand towards the house. Tabby hobbled back hurriedly indoors to get dressed, her brain struggling to encompass what she had seen at the same time as she accepted that, yet again, the very foundations of her relationship with the man she had married had been demolished and everything had changed.

Sexual desire had stimulated that change, she conceded, shame slivering through her. *No boundaries*, Acheron had proclaimed with passion and he was certainly correct on that score: the rules she had tried to impose had been blown right out of the water along with her nonsensical belief that she could resist him. Even more pertinently, seeing Melinda touch Acheron had inflamed her with ferocious possessiveness and the sort of angry jealous feelings she had never before experienced. What did that say about her intelligence? What was she letting him do to her? Where were these violent conflicting emotions coming from? She was behaving like a lovesick idiot! Was that the problem? Had lust first sucked her in and then left her childishly infatuated with him?

Opening her as yet still packed cases, she extracted underwear and a long, loose sundress before stepping into the bathroom to freshen up. The whole process took her much longer than usual having to wash her hair in the sink, which was a challenge, and left the bathroom floor swimming by the time she had finished. When she finally emerged after mopping dry the floor, however, she felt more like herself with clean, tidy hair and a little make-up applied.

Acheron strolled into the bedroom and there Tabby was; captured in a patch of sunlight, long golden hair rippling down to softly frame her delicate features, her tiny body sylphlike in a pale blue dress that reflected her amazing eyes, which were currently pools of anxious troubled violet that evaded his. She was *so* open, *so* honest in her reactions, it literally shocked him. Nothing was concealed; nothing was hidden from him. His broad chest tightened as he expelled his breath and gritted his teeth. He could not begin to imagine how frighteningly vulnerable that lack of concealment and reserve made her. If he didn't act first, she was undoubtedly about to unleash a rash volley of accusations and questions about their renewed intimacy, which threatened to put them both right back where they had started after their car crash wedding night and her proclamation of her unnecessary rules.

'Tabby,' he murmured evenly, noting avidly that he could see the little points of her deliciously prominent nipples showing below the fine material of her dress as well as the slender outline of her shapely legs. An overpoweringly strong urge to claim her again assailed him.

'Ash,' she said breathlessly, studying his lean, darkly handsome features with a sinking heart because that fast she was out of breath and dizzy just looking at him. 'We need to talk.'

'No, we don't, *glyka mou*,' Acheron contradicted with stubborn assurance as he drew closer. 'Let's do this my way. We don't talk, we especially *don't* agonise over anything. It is what it is and we just enjoy it for as long as it lasts.'

He had snatched the confused words out of her mouth before she had even collected her thoughts enough to speak. She suspected that his solution was vintage Acheron in the field of relationships—say nothing, do nothing and the problem will go away. 'I wasn't about to agonise over anything,' she protested, swaying slightly because she found it hard to stand still for long and had to grip the walking stick in a tighter hold.

He closed hands round her forearms to steady her and slowly trailed his hands down to her waist. 'You can't help yourself.'

As she looked up at him, her lush full lips tingled and she was conscious of a sensation like prickling heat curling low in her pelvis. He angled his mouth down and kissed her with intoxicating urgency.

'Oh…' she said in breathless surprise at the development, her body humming into ready awareness with an enthusiasm that disconcerted her.

He lifted her dress slowly, brazen dark golden eyes locked to hers, daring her to object. Anticipation pierced her, sharp as a lance, liquid heat pooling between her thighs. His gaze not once leaving hers, he found her with his fingers, eased below her lace-edged panties and stroked and that fast she was hotter than the fires of hell, leaning up against him for support, making no objection when he gently lowered her back onto the bed. The stick fell forgotten on the floor.

'I only just got up,' she exclaimed, her surprise unconcealed.

'You should've waited here for me, *glyka mou*,' Acheron told her sibilantly.

'I can't believe you want me again already.' Tabby studied him with confused and wondering eyes.

'The instant I look at you I want you,' Acheron admitted in a slightly raw undertone because there was a lack of control and a weakness in such a truth that deeply disturbed him.

'Not the very first time you saw me,' she reminded him stubbornly.

'You swore at me...not your finest hour, *glyka mou*,' he mocked. 'Now that I know you, it wouldn't bother me at all or make me stop thinking that you're the hottest woman on the planet.'

Eyes wide with astonishment, Tabby was transfixed by that statement. 'You really mean that?'

'*You have to ask*? Here I am throwing you down on the bed to ravish and you have to ask how much I want you? I can't wait to get you horizontal and that's not OK,' Acheron groaned, yanking off her panties with scant ceremony and splaying her legs with a voracious hiss of all-male satisfaction, fully appreciating the pink glistening femininity he had exposed. 'No, don't spoil the view,' he censured when, hot-cheeked, she tried to scissor her thighs together again. 'I like to look and I *love* to appreciate.'

Tabby forced herself to remember that while he peeled off his trunks, revealing his long, thick erection. Heat rolled through her, moisture gathering at the heart of her along with a soul-deep yearning that should have terrified her. She realised that she was acting on instinct, not even pausing to think about what he had said, skipping the *agonising* as he had phrased it because what woman wished to be viewed in that light?

'*Thee mou*, hot, hot, hot,' Acheron rasped as he came down on top of her, punctuating every word with a passionate kiss and hands that traced every erogenous zone she possessed until her impatience steadily rose to match his.

Only then did he sink into her hard and fast, muttering something in Greek before he paused to press his lips to her brow. 'Am I hurting you?' he grated uneasily.

'Only if you stop,' she traded helplessly, her whole body clenching round him as possessively as her arms, hands smoothing over his satin-smooth back, clenching there, nails curving inward as he ground into her, and she cried out in helpless delight. Excitement rose in an unstoppable tide, and she lost the self she knew in it, living from one glorious moment of intense sensation to the next until the great gathering storm became too much to contain and the passion swept her off the heights down into the ecstatic rippling aftermath.

'Well, there wasn't much finesse about that,' Acheron remarked, cradling her up against him in a damp tangle of limbs. 'My apologies.'

'No need,' Tabby countered, pressing her mouth softly to his chest, revelling in the hot, musky smell of his skin and the closeness that he was embracing. 'It was another ten out of ten.'

'You're *grading* me now?' he demanded in obvious horror.

'If you drop down to a five or lower, I'll warn you,' Tabby teased, smiling because she felt amazingly light-hearted while she was studiously engaged in not agonising. The minute she forgot his maxim though the real world immediately flooded back and, assailed by those whirling doubts, insecurities and unanswered questions, she became tense again and marvelled that she had so easily suppressed what she had seen.

'I saw you with Melinda on the beach,' she told him baldly, putting it right out there without holding back and judging her words and their effect.

Acheron's big powerful frame stiffened and he tilted her head back to study her troubled face. 'I'm bringing another nanny in to work with Melinda, who will eventually replace her. I've already made the arrangements. I don't want Amber upset by too sudden a change in staff,' he volunteered.

Tabby was wildly disconcerted by the announcement but relieved to know that Melinda would soon be moving on, while being impressed and touched that he had also been careful to consider Amber's need for consistent care. 'You're planning to sack Melinda?'

'She's on a temporary contract. We can let her go any time we like but I'd prefer to dispense with her services in the usual way. She knows a little too much about our marriage for my comfort.'

Frowning at that admission, Tabby prompted, 'What do you mean?'

'Melinda is clearly aware that we were using separate bedrooms at the villa. When we were on the beach she offered to share Amber's room so that I could take over hers,' Acheron explained grimly.

Wings of hot pink reddened Tabby's cheeks. Annoyance and embarrassment that their unconventional sleeping arrangements had evidently attracted the attention of the staff engulfed her. 'Perhaps she was planning to do a little wandering during the night once you were conveniently close. She *was* coming on to you, wasn't she?'

Lean, extravagantly handsome features impassive, stunning dark eyes screened, Acheron nodded. 'It happens.'

Tabby looked up at him, weak with relief that he had told her the truth without fanfare or fuss. 'Often?'

Acheron released a rueful chuckle at the innocence of that question. 'All the time. If I ignore it, it usually dies a natural death but Melinda doesn't take hints…possibly because she's already reached the conclusion that ours is not a normal marriage. She *could* take that information to the press, laying me open to a potential charge that I only married you to circumvent my father's will.'

Tabby grimaced. 'We'll have to work harder at being a more convincing couple. Share a room, spend time together, fake it up to behave more like a honeymoon couple is expected to behave.'

'But it doesn't have to be fake now,' Acheron pointed out with lazy assurance.

But in her heart she would know it *was* fake, Tabby reflected painfully. He gave her great sex but he wasn't offering to give her anything more. Maybe that was the only kind of giving he knew—short-term physical stuff with a built-in time limit, she conceded fairly, not wanting to judge him just because he was different. After all, was she any more evolved in the field of relationships? She wanted him *so* much, wanted his attention as much as Amber did, was willing to do whatever it took to hold that attention. But she was not willing to admit even to herself that he was also stirring up emotions that she was afraid she couldn't handle.

'Why did your father write a will that forced you to get married when you didn't want to?' Tabby asked quietly, knowing that that was the heart of the matter and the mystery that he had so far avoided explaining.

'In a nutshell? He wanted me to marry Kasma,' Acheron told her tersely, his beautiful mouth hardening. 'And I don't *ever* want to talk about that.'

With difficulty, Tabby swallowed an irritated comeback on that omission, knowing such a response would only reinforce his reserve and make him dig his stubborn heels in even harder. She could leave the thorny question of Kasma to one side for the moment and concentrate on other aspects. 'But surely your father knew how you felt? How close were the two of you?' Tabby persisted.

A tiny muscle pulled taut at the corner of his unsmiling jaw. 'I only met him in my late twenties,' he reminded her drily. 'I suppose it was more of a business relationship than most. His company was struggling. He asked me for advice. I went in to help and ended up taking over.'

'Didn't he resent that?'

'Not at all. He wasn't much of a businessman, more of a family man desperate to give his loved ones a secure future.'

'That was your stepmother and her children?'

Acheron compressed his lips. 'My father married her when her kids were very young and raised them as his own but I didn't meet them until about eighteen months before he died.'

'Why not?' Tabby asked in surprise.

'His family weren't relevant to me or to our relationship. They were strangers. There was no blood tie and I've never had a family, so I was very wary about getting involved in that side of his life. As things turned out, I was right to be wary and to have kept my distance for as long as I did,' he pronounced with dark finality.

A silence full of undertones enclosed them in the aftermath of that assurance, adding to Tabby's discomfiture. She was trying desperately to work out what his past relationship with his stepsister, Kasma, had entailed. Obviously there had been an affair that left the beautiful brunette with expectations that Acheron was not prepared to fulfil. Presumably the affair had ended badly with bitterness on both sides. Had some tragedy occurred? Had Kasma fallen pregnant or some such thing? Mightn't that explain why his late father had got such a bee in his bonnet about Acheron marrying his stepdaughter? Certainly the other woman had believed very strongly that she was the only woman who should become Acheron's wife. Was Kasma in love with him? Or was she more fixated on his money and his status? But regardless of why Kasma wanted Acheron, what did it matter when *he* didn't want *her*? Tabby asked herself irritably, weary of suspicions that were winding up her tension for no good reason. If it was that simple though, why couldn't he just say so?

'I wish you didn't keep secrets. I wish you were more frank and straightforward about things,' she admitted before she could think better of it.

'You're so honest sometimes you terrify me, *glyka mou*,' Acheron confided ruefully. 'And if this honeymoon is going to work, we will each have to compromise our most cherished ideals.'

Acheron peered down at the red-rose tattoo adorning Tabby's slender arm with a frown and stroked a finger gently across it. 'The skin underneath feels rough and the design is already blurred. The tattooist must have damaged your skin.'

Tabby gritted her teeth, relaxation abandoned as she yanked her arm free of his light hold. 'Don't touch me there.'

Lustrous dark golden eyes scrutinised her from below inky-black lashes. 'Why not?'

'Are we about to have *another* one of those conversations in which you suggest that I go for laser treatment to have it removed?' Tabby condemned, her small face taut and pale as she decided it was time to tell him the truth, which would surely conclude his interest in the subject. 'If you must know, I won't have it removed because it's covering up an ugly scar. In fact, the scar was there first. The tattooist did a marvellous job but he couldn't have made the ink design perfect when my skin was far from perfect to begin with.'

His lean dark features were frowning now. 'What sort of a scar?'

'Take it from me...you really don't want to know,' Tabby told him warningly, pulling away from him to scramble to her feet in the shade of the pine trees that overhung the pinkish pale sand. After checking that Amber still lay splayed out on her blanket in sleeping abandonment, her olive-skinned chubby limbs protruding starfish fashion from her white *broderie anglaise* play-suit, her rosebud mouth soft and relaxed, Tabby stalked on down the beach, a slight figure clad in shorts and a bikini top.

Acheron, she thought, her hands knotting into fists, her teeth grinding together in angry frustration. There were times she wanted to throw him into the sea from a great height. She had thought *she* was the nosy one but he didn't quit once he was on a trail either. Even worse, he was a domineering perfectionist. Although he wasn't planning to spend the rest of his life with her and Amber, he still wanted to persuade her that she should have the tattoo removed and he was as relentless as a steam roller running down a hill. At breakfast he had asked her if she would be happy for Amber to get something similar done, and Tabby had been betrayed into looking in dismay at Amber's smooth soft forearm and Acheron, being Acheron, had noticed that revealing appraisal.

'So, you *do* regret getting it done,' he had exclaimed with satisfaction.

Yes, Acheron had some infuriating traits, she acknowledged, but over the past month in Sardinia he had also been a highly entertaining companion, a very sexy lover and a patient and caring father figure for Amber. At that moment, Tabby couldn't begin to work out how an entire four weeks had flashed past faster than the speed of light. The first week had been a challenge while she was still hobbling round with a stick and pretty much sentenced to passing her time at the beach house. But once her ankle had healed, they had begun to go out and about.

Snapshots of special moments they had shared filled her memory with more comforting images. They had climbed the massive staircase to the Bastione terrace to see the amazing panoramic view of the rooftops of Calgiari. While she was still wheezing from the climb and overheated from the sun, he had told her that there was actually a lift but that he had assumed that she would enjoy the full tourist experience more. It had taken several cocktails and the cooling effect of the lovely breeze on the terrace before she had forgiven him, and if she was truthful her resistance had only truly melted when he slid long brown fingers into hers in the lift on the way down again.

They had made an evening visit to Castelsardo, a beautiful village dominated by a magical citadel all lit up at night, to enjoy live music in the piazza. Amber had adored all the noise and bustle going on around her and Acheron had enjoyed the baby's bright-eyed fascination.

The following night, however, they had sought out more adult fun, dancing until dawn at the Billionaire club where Tabby had felt distinctly overshadowed by the number of gorgeous women, sleek and deadly as sharks, cruising for a wealthy hook-up. That Ash had acted as if he only had eyes for her and had kissed her passionately on the dance floor had done much to lift her self-esteem.

Memory after memory was now tumbling inside Tabby's head. For forty-eight hours they had sailed a yacht round the national park of La Maddalena, a group of protected and largely uninhabited islands teeming with flora and wildlife. The last night they had skinny dipped in a deserted cove and made love until the sun went down. Exhausted, she had wakened to find Acheron barbecuing their evening meal, stunning dark golden eyes smiling lazily at her and making her heart somersault like a trapeze artist.

Of course, they had done all the usual things as well, like strolling round the famous boutiques on the Costa Smeralda, an activity or a lack of activity that Acheron was astounded to discover bored his bride to tears.

'But you *must* want me to buy you something,' he had protested. 'You *must* have seen something you liked. You do realise that the only thing I've bought you since we arrived is that bed linen?'

Tabby had seen the exquisite bed linen in an up-market handicrafts shop and her childhood memories of being clumsy with a needle and thread had given her a true appreciation of the amount of skill involved in producing such beautiful embroidery. That had been a purchase to treasure, a gift she truly loved, and only later had it occurred to her that she would never see that winter-weight linen spread across a bed that she shared with Acheron and that it would inevitably adorn a bed she slept in alone. Once the summer was over, their marriage would be history.

But then while she had known they would be faking their honeymoon and had dutifully posed with him for a persistent paparazzo, who had followed them round Porto Cervo, she had not appreciated the lengths Acheron might go to in making their relationship look genuine from the inside and the outside. So, if occasionally she got a little confused and thought about him as if he *were* her real husband, who could blame her for making that mistake?

Or for falling madly and irrevocably in love with him during the process, she reasoned wretchedly.

After all, no man had ever treated her as well as he did, no man had ever made her so happy either, and only he had ever made love to her several times a day, *every* day, as if she were indeed the hottest, sexiest woman on the planet. Naturally her emotions had got involved and she suppressed them as best she could, knowing that the last thing Acheron required from her was angst and a broken heart, which would make him feel guilty and uncomfortable.

It wasn't his fault she had fallen for him either. It certainly wasn't as though he had misled her with promises about the future. In fact, right from the outset she had known that there was no future for them. He had never made any bones about that. Once they had succeeded to legally adopt Amber, their supposed marriage would be left to wither and die. Tabby would make a new life with the little girl she loved while she assumed Acheron would return to his workaholic, womanising existence. Would she ever see him again after the divorce? As she confronted that bleak prospect an agonising shard of pain slivered through Tabby and left a deep anguished ache in its wake. Would Acheron want to retain even the most distant relationship with Amber? Or would he decide on a clean break and act as if Amber didn't exist?

Acheron crossed the beach, noting how Tabby's figure had rounded out once she was eating decent food, recalling with quiet satisfaction that she no longer bit her nails—small changes that he valued.

'How did you get the scar concealed by the tattoo?' he demanded obstinately, interrupting Tabby's reverie and shooting her back to the present by wrapping both arms round her from behind, carefully preventing her from storming off again. 'Were you involved in an accident?'

'No…it wasn't an accident,' Tabby admitted, past recollections making her skin turn suddenly cold and clammy in spite of the heat of the sun.

He was being supportive, she reminded herself doggedly, guilt biting into her former annoyance with him. When Amber had cried half the night because she was teething and her gums were sore, Acheron had been right there beside her, helping to distract the little girl and calm her down enough to sleep again. She had not expected supportiveness from Acheron but his interest in Amber was anything but half-hearted. When it came to childcare, he took the rough with the smooth, serenely accepting that children weren't always sunny and smiling.

The new nanny currently working with Melinda was called Teresa, a warm, chattering Italian woman whose main source of interest was her charge. Within a week the English nanny would be leaving to take up a permanent position with a family in London.

'Tabby...I asked you a question,' Acheron reminded her with deeply unwelcome persistence. 'You said you didn't get the scar in an accident, so—'

Dredged from the teeming tumult of her frantic attempt to think about just about anything other than the past he was trying to dig up, Tabby lifted her head high and looked out to sea. 'My mother burned me with a hot iron because I knocked over a carton of milk,' she confessed without any expression at all.

'*Thee mou...*' Acheron growled in stricken disbelief, spinning her round to look at her pale set face and the yawning hurt still lingering in her violet eyes.

'I was never allowed to be with either of my parents unsupervised again after that,' she explained woodenly. 'My mother went to prison for burning me and I never saw either of them again.'

Bewildered by the great surge of ferocious anger welling up inside him, Acheron crushed her slight body to his, both arms wrapping tightly round her. For some reason he registered that he was feeling sick and his hands weren't quite steady, and in that instant some inexplicable deep need that disturbed him was making it impossible for him not to touch her. 'That must've been a relief.'

'No, it wasn't. I loved them. They weren't very lovable people but they were all I had,' Tabby admitted thickly, her dry throat scratching over the words as if she was reluctant to voice them. She had learned as a young child that loving gestures would be rejected but now more than anything in the world she wanted to wrap her arms round Acheron and take full advantage of the comfort he was clumsily trying to offer her, only that pattern of early rejection and knowledge of how abandonment felt kept her body rigid and uninviting in the circle of his arms.

'I understand that,' Acheron breathed in a raw driven undertone. 'I rarely saw my mother but I still idolised her—'

'What a pair we are!' Tabby sniffed, her tension suddenly giving way as tears stung her eyes and overflowed, her overloaded reaction to having had to explain and indeed relive what she never, ever talked about to anyone.

Acheron stared down at her tear-stained visage, pale below his bronzed skin, his strong facial bones forbiddingly set. 'I can't bear to think of you being hurt like that, *yineka mou*—'

'Don't...don't talk about it!' Tabby urged feverishly. 'I try never to think about it but every time I saw the scar in the mirror as a teenager, I remembered it, and sometimes people asked what had happened to me. That's why I got the tattoo... to cover it up, hide it.'

'Then wear that tattoo with pride. It's a survival badge,' Acheron informed her with hard satisfaction. 'I wish you'd explained weeks ago but I understand now why you didn't.'

'Oh, for goodness' sake, let's talk about something more cheerful!' Tabby pleaded. 'Tell me something about you. I mean, you must have *some* happy childhood memories of your mother?'

Acheron closed an arm round her slight shoulders to press her back across the beach towards Amber. 'The night before my first day at school she presented me with a fantastically expensive pen engraved with my name. Of course, I was only allowed to use a pencil in class but naturally that didn't occur to her. She was very fond of flamboyant gestures, always telling me that only the very best was good enough for a Dimitrakos—'

'Maybe that was how she was brought up,' Tabby suggested quietly. 'But you still haven't explained why that pen made you happy.'

'Because generally she ignored me but that particular week she was fresh out of rehab and engaged in turning over a new leaf and it was the one and only time she made me feel that I genuinely mattered to her. She even gave me a whole speech about education being the most important thing in my life…that from a woman who dropped out of school as a teenager and couldn't read anything more challenging than a magazine,' he told her wryly.

'Do you still have the pen?'

'I think it was stolen.' He sent her a rueful charismatic smile that tilted her heart inside her chest and interfered with her breathing. 'But at least I have that one perfect moment to remember her by.'

Acheron could not relax until he had commissioned a special piece of jewellery for Tabby's upcoming birthday, which surprisingly fell in the same week as his own. That achieved, he worried about having taken that much trouble over a gift. What was wrong with him? What sort of man went to such lengths for a wife he was planning to divorce? *Keep it cool*, a little voice chimed in the back of his uneasy mind. But it had proved impossible to play it cool when confronted with the harsh reality of Tabby's childhood experiences, which had had the unexpected effect of showing

Acheron that he had a good deal less to be bitter about with regard to his own. His mother had been a neglectful, selfish and inadequate parent but even at her worst he had never doubted that she loved him. And possibly, but for the malicious machinations of a third party, his father might have learned to love and appreciate him as well…

The constant flow of such unfamiliar thoughts assailing him kept him quiet over dinner. Aware of Tabby's anxious gaze, he was maddened by the knowledge that he wasn't feeling like himself any more and that, even in the midst of that disorientating experience, withdrawing his attention from her could make him feel guilty. Never a fan of great inner debates, or even in the habit of staging them, he was exasperated and bewildered by the emotions Tabby constantly churned up inside him. *She was too intense*, too rich for his blood. He needed to take a step back, he decided abruptly; he needed some distance, and the instant he made that decision he felt better and back in control again.

'I have to go away on business for a couple of days,' Acheron volunteered as he strode out of the bathroom, a towel negligently wrapped round his lean, muscular body. His black hair tousled and damp, his lean, devastatingly handsome face clean-shaven, he looked amazing and Tabby's mouth ran dry before she could even process what he had said.

Realising that he was leaving her, Tabby went rigid and then scolded herself because he had done very little work in recent weeks and could hardly be expected to maintain that lifestyle indefinitely. No, she had been spoilt by his constant company and had to learn fast how to adapt to his absence. Was that why he had been so quiet and distant over dinner? Had he worried about her reaction? Well, it was time to show him that she was strong and not the complaining type.

'I'll miss you, but we'll be fine,' she responded lightly.

Acheron ground his teeth together, having expected her to object or even offer to travel with him. This was definitely a moment when he had believed she would cling and make him feel suffocated. He watched her clamber into bed, slender as a willow wand, the modest nightdress concealing the hot, secret places he loved, and lust kicked in so fast he felt dizzy with it. Lustrous dark eyes veiling, he discarded the towel, doused the lights and joined her. *Not tonight*, he thought grimly, as though he was fighting a battle; tonight he could get by without her.

Eyes sparkling in the moonlight, Tabby rolled over to Acheron's side of the bed and ran delicate fingers hungrily across a hair-roughened thigh while her hair trailed over his pelvis.

Acheron closed his eyes in despair. He could always lie back and think of Greece. If he said no like a frightened virgin, he would probably upset her, and there was no point doing that, was there? Why risk upsetting her? She found his swelling shaft with her mouth, and his hips shifted upward in helpless encouragement. It crossed his mind that the divorce might upset her because she acted as if she was fond of him, looked at him as if he was special, dived on him in bed if he didn't dive on her first, never missed a chance to put her arms round him…although strangely *not* this afternoon on the beach when he had put his arms round her in an effort to offer sympathy for what his thoughtless questions had made her cruelly relive. A particularly strong wave of pleasure blanked out the subsequent thought about *why* she might not have responded, yet another thought he didn't want to have. All that sentimental stuff, he thought grimly—he never had been any good at that. He had probably been clumsy.

Afterwards, Acheron didn't hold her the way he usually did, and Tabby felt cold inside and abandoned. She curled up on her side, hating him, loving him, wanting him, fretting and reckoning that love was the worst torture in existence for a woman. There was no point always wanting what he wouldn't give her, didn't even *want* to give her, she reflected painfully. Their divorce was not only written in the stars but also written into a pre-nuptial contract from which there would be no escape.

And maybe he still had feelings for Kasma, whom he would not discuss although she had on several occasions worked the conversation helpfully round in that direction to give him an easy opening. But trying to get Acheron to talk about something he didn't want to talk about was like trying to get blood out of a stone. In her experience though, people only avoided topics that embarrassed or troubled them, so his failed relationship with Kasma must have gone deep indeed to leave behind such conspicuous and quite uncharacteristic sensitivity…

The following morning, Tabby drifted out of sleep to discover that Acheron had made an early departure and without leaving even a note. She spent a quiet day with Amber and it was the next day before the silence from Acheron began to niggle at her. He didn't have to stay in touch when he was only planning to be away forty-eight hours, she conceded ruefully, and she was not so needy that she required him to check in with her every day. But as she lay in the bed that felt empty without him the day stretched before Tabby like a blank slate, shorn of anticipation, excitement and happiness.

Thoroughly exasperated with her mood, she went for a shower and got dressed in the bathroom, emerging to catch a glimpse of her reflection in the tall cheval mirror across the bedroom and wonder why she couldn't see it properly. As she automatically moved closer to see what was amiss with the mirror she realised that someone had written something on it, and she frowned at it in bewilderment.

He's using you! Tabby was gobsmacked. Why would anyone write that on their mirror for her to see? Clearly it was meant to be personal, and presumably Acheron was the 'he' being referred to. What on earth did it mean? Whatever, it really spooked her that someone had come into their bedroom while she was in the bathroom and left a message presumably intended to shock and insult her. After all, only someone in the house could have had access to their room and that knowledge made gooseflesh blossom on her exposed skin.

Without hesitation she lifted the house phone and asked to speak to Ash's security chief, Dmitri. Almost before she had finished speaking, Dmitri joined her in the room to see the mirror for himself. If his forbidding expression was anything to go by, he took the matter very seriously. Dmitri, however, was a man of few words and she left him to it and went downstairs for breakfast.

CHAPTER TEN

'CAN I ASK you where you're planning to go?' Melinda asked with a sunny smile, joining her at the breakfast table, which she never dared to do when Acheron was around.

'Into Porto Cervo to shop,' Tabby admitted. 'I'm looking for a birthday present.'

'There's some great jewellery boutiques…try the Piazzetta delle Chiacchere,' Melinda advised helpfully.

Tabby nodded, feeling guilty about how much she disliked the curvaceous blonde who would, by the end of the week, mercifully be gone from the household to take up her new appointment. Since Teresa's arrival and increasing involvement with Amber, Melinda seemed to spend a lot of time hovering unnecessarily and watching their comings and goings. Once, Tabby had even suspected that the blonde was eavesdropping on her and Acheron. No doubt the nanny had now registered that their detached marriage had developed into something closer. Or was that only her own wishful thinking at work? Tabby wondered heavily.

Acheron had been gone only one day and she felt bereft. That was a pretty poor show for a strong, independent woman, she conceded shame-facedly. She missed him so much, and her outlook wasn't improved by her recollection of his unusual behaviour on that last night they had spent together. He had been silent and moody, extraordinarily uninvolved when she had made love to him, saying nothing, doing nothing, in fact, acting like a right—

'Miss Barnes?' Dmitri appeared in the doorway. 'Could I have a word with you?'

'*Right* now?' Melinda prompted with a sparkling smile that seemed wasted on the granite-faced older man.

'Now would be a good time,' Dmitri responded evenly.

Tabby left Teresa in charge of Amber, having decided that dragging the little girl out to trail round the shops during the hottest part of the day would be unwise. The message was still on the mirror when she walked past into the bathroom to renew her lipstick and it made her shiver. *He's using you.* Well, as far as their marriage was concerned they were using each other, she told herself doggedly. Although things had changed drastically once they began sharing a bed in reality. Was Acheron only sleeping with her because that intimacy added to the illusion of their having a normal marriage? After all, if he was seen out by the paparazzi with another woman while he was supposed to be a happily married new husband, it wouldn't look good. So, was she being used on that basis? But how could she call it using when she was in love with him and wanted him to make love to her? Did that make her a silly lovelorn fool? Or was *she* taking equal advantage of *him*?

From the instant Dmitri phoned him and broke the news, Acheron hadn't been able to stay still or think with his usual logic. Gripped by insane impatience and mounting concern, he just wanted to get back to Sardinia and stand watch over Tabby and Amber. Unfortunately for him, getting a last-minute slot for the jet to take off in Athens and jumping the queue took longer than he had envisaged. He cursed the fact that he had left them behind in the first place, cursed his conviction that he should protect Tabby at all costs from what Kasma might do next.

Why had he chosen to leave Tabby when he actually wanted to be with her? What did that say about him? That he couldn't recognise his own emotions and was prone to running away from what he couldn't understand? Feelings had never been so intense for him before and he had been torn between a kind of intoxication at the fire of them and a kind of panic at knowing he was out of control. He had never allowed that to happen to him before but he'd had no choice. He had jumped on the panic as an excuse and now he was paying the price. Thee mou, *if anything was to happen to them*, he brooded darkly, his fists clenching aggressively just as his pilot signalled him from across the VIP lounge that they were good to go.

'I really do believe that your husband would prefer you to stay in today,' Dmitri informed Tabby quietly.

Unfortunately, Tabby was in no mood to be grounded like a child and marvelled that Acheron could even think he could give out orders that way through Dmitri, particularly when he had taken off himself at such short notice. What was it? Why was he trying to keep her on the home front? Some sort of control issue on his part? And poor Dmitri was embarrassed to have to say such a thing to her; she could see it in the older man.

'I'm sorry but it's really important that I go out today,' she said levelly. 'I have something I have to buy.'

'Then I'll accompany you and I'll drive, Mrs Dimitrakos,' Dmitri responded with determination.

For the sake of peace, Tabby nodded agreement but knew she was going to have to have a discussion with Acheron with regard to the intense security presence he maintained in their lives. Was it really necessary that they be guarded and watched over every place they went? Was there a genuine risk of their being robbed or kidnapped? Was there some kind of specific threat out against Acheron?

'You'll be very bored,' she warned Dmitri as she settled into the passenger seat of the SUV and watched another car full of security men follow them out of the entrance to the beach house with wry acceptance.

'It's not a problem. I'm used to going shopping with my wife,' Dmitri told her calmly. 'She can stare at one shop window for ten minutes before she's satisfied she's seen everything.'

Tabby knew she would be even more of a drag because she didn't even know what she was planning to buy and was hoping to be inspired by something she saw. What did you buy for the man who had everything? The massive monthly allowance he had awarded her, however, had piled up in her bank account and thanks to his generosity she had got to spend very little of it, so she had plenty to spend.

Dmitri following behind her, Tabby prowled through the exclusive boutiques and jewellery outlets. Acheron wasn't the sort of guy who wore jewellery. He wore a wedding ring and occasionally cuff links and that was all. But short of copping out by buying him another silk tie when he already had a rail of them, what was she to give him for his thirty-first birthday? Mulling over that thorny issue, she saw the pen. Actually *the* pen was the only possible description for a pen that bore a world-famous designer label. It would cost a fortune, she reckoned. But equally fast she recalled the pen his mother had bought him and decided that the cost was less important than what it meant, although why she was so keen to buy a significant gift for a man who couldn't even be bothered to phone her, she couldn't explain. Maybe it was the desolate thought that the pen might survive with him a lot longer than their marriage and act as a reminder of what they had once shared. Depressing, much? She scolded herself impatiently for her downbeat thoughts.

She bought the pen and arranged for it to be inscribed with his name and the date. She had to make use of the platinum credit card he had given her to make the purchase and, while trying to act as if she spent such sums all the time, she was secretly horrified at spending so much money and worried that Acheron would think she had gone mad. Pale and shaken after that sobering experience, she told Dmitri that she wanted to go for a coffee. He led the way to an outdoor café and insisted on choosing a seat a couple of tables away from her.

She had just bought the most expensive pen in the history of the world, she reflected guiltily, and when he saw the bill he might well freak out and regret telling her that her card had no upper limit. She was sipping her latte slowly, savouring the caffeine, when a shadow fell across her table.

Kasma settled her long elegant body down smoothly into the seat opposite. 'You've been so unavailable you've forced me into all this cloak and dagger stuff,' she complained.

Totally taken aback by the other woman's appearance, Tabby stared at the beautiful brunette with wide, questioning eyes. 'What on earth are you doing here?'

'You're here, Ash is here…where else would I be?' Kasma asked, rolling big dark eyes in apparent disbelief at the question. 'I refuse to believe that you're so stupid that you can't accept that Ash belongs with me.'

'Miss Philippides…' Dmitri broke into the conversation, standing straight and tall beside Kasma's chair. 'Please leave—'

Kasma slung him a defiant glance. 'We're in a public place and I can go where I please on this island. We're not in Greece now.'

'May I suggest then that *we* leave, Mrs Dimitrakos?' Dmitri continued, regarding Tabby expectantly.

Tabby breathed in deep. 'When I've finished my coffee,' she murmured, determined to hear what Kasma had to say since she sure as heck wasn't going to receive any information from Acheron.

Grim-faced, Dmitri retreated to an even closer table.

'I believe in getting straight down to business,' Kasma informed her. 'How much money do you want to walk out on this absurd marriage?'

Dumbstruck, Tabby stared at the older woman. 'You can't be serious.'

'Oh, I'm always serious when it comes to Ash. We belong together and he would have married me, *not* you, had my stepfather not foolishly tried to force the issue in his will,' Kasma contended confidently. 'You must know how proud Ash is.'

'Staying here, entering into this dialogue is a very bad idea, Mrs Dimitrakos,' Dmitri leant closer to spell out.

Kasma shot a vicious burst of Greek at the older man and the look on her face was downright scary. With the sudden suspicion that Dmitri's advice to retreat from the scene might well be the most sensible move, Tabby lifted her bag, settled some money on the table for the bill and stood up. Before she walked away, however, she had something to say. 'No matter how much money you offered me I wouldn't walk out on Acheron,' she murmured tautly. 'I love him.'

'Not as much as I love him, you bitch!' Kasma launched at her in a seething shout of fury that shook Tabby rigid.

Cupping her elbow firmly in his hand, Dmitri walked her away from the café at a fast pace. 'Kasma Philippides is a dangerously unstable woman. Your husband has a restraining order out against her on Greek soil and she's not allowed to approach him or make a nuisance of herself there. You can't talk to her. You can't reason with her. We've learned that the hard way.'

'Ash should've warned me. If he'd warned me, I would've walked away immediately,' Tabby protested defensively. 'I could see that she was obsessed with him at the wedding but I didn't understand how much of a problem she was in his life.'

'He wasn't expecting her to follow you here. He had no idea she was on the island. By the way, he's flying back as we speak.'

Relief swept Tabby. He would finally have to tell her the whole story. But he had had to take out a legal restraining order to keep Kasma at a distance? What had driven him to take his father's stepdaughter to court? That must have taken some nerve, particularly while his father was still alive. Had Kasma been acting like some sort of psycho stalker?

They were driving along the coast road when she noticed that Dmitri kept on looking worriedly in the driving mirror. Tabby glanced over her shoulder to notice the bright red sports car behind them. The driver had long dark hair just like Kasma's.

'She's following us,' Dmitri told her flatly.

'Make sure your belt is safely fastened. I may have to take evasive manoeuvres but I've already alerted the police.'

'Evasive manoeuvres?' Tabby gasped when there was a sudden jolt at the rear of the car. 'She's trying to ram us? Is she crazy in that tiny little car?'

Dmitri didn't answer. His concentration was on the road because he had speeded up. Tabby's heart was beating very, very fast as she watched in the mirror as the red car tried to catch up with them again. They were zooming round corners so fast that Tabby felt dizzy and she was still watching Kasma's car when it veered across the road into the path of another car travelling the other way.

'Oh, my word, she's crashed…hit someone else!'

Dmitri jammed on the brakes and rammed into Reverse to turn and drive back. He leapt out of the SUV. The team from the other security car were already attending to the victims of the crash, carrying the passenger to the verge, the driver, still conscious, stumbling after them. The red sports car had hit a wall and demolished part of it. Tabby slowly climbed out, her tummy heaving as she approached the scene of frantic activity. Dmitri was talking fast on his phone as he approached her. 'Stay in the car, Mrs Dimitrakos. You don't need to see this. Miss Philippides is dead.'

'Dead?' Tabby was stunned, barely able to credit that the woman who had been speaking to her only minutes earlier could have lost her life.

'She wasn't wearing a belt—she was thrown from the car.'

'And the people who were in the other car?' Tabby asked.

'Very lucky to be alive. The passenger has a head wound and the driver has a leg injury.'

Tabby nodded and got back slowly into the SUV, feeling oddly distanced from everything happening around her. That sensation, which she only vaguely recognised as shock, was still lingering when she gave a brief statement at the police station with a lawyer sitting in, volunteering information she couldn't understand in the local language. That completed, she was stowed in a waiting room with a cup of coffee until Acheron strode through the door. He stalked across the room, emanating stormy tension, and raised her out of her seat with two anxious hands.

'You are all right? Dmitri swore you were unhurt but I was afraid to believe him,' Acheron grated half under his breath, his lean, darkly handsome features taut and granite hard as he scanned her carefully from head to toe.

'Well, I was fine until you made me spill my coffee,' she responded unevenly, setting the mug down and rubbing ineffectually at the splashes now adorning her pale pink top. 'Are we free to leave?'

'Yes, I've made a statement. *Thee mou*,' Acheron murmured fiercely. 'Kasma had a knife in her bag!'

'A *knife*?' Tabby repeated in horror.

'But for Dmitri's presence she might have attacked you!' Acheron lifted a not quite steady hand and raked long brown fingers through his luxuriant black hair. 'I was so scared when I heard she'd come here, I felt sick,' he confided thickly.

'She's dead,' Tabby reminded him in an undertone.

Acheron released his pent-up breath and said heavily, 'Her brother, Simeon, is on his way to make the funeral arrangements. He's a decent man. I hope you don't mind but I've asked him to stay with us.'

'Of course, I don't mind. No matter what's happened, your father's family deserve your consideration and respect.'

'Melinda's flying back to London,' Acheron volunteered. 'She was responsible for the messages on the mirror.'

'Messages…there was *more* than one?' Tabby queried in consternation.

Acheron told her about the message he had seen at the villa in Tuscany and how Dmitri had instantly worked out that Melinda had to be the perpetrator when the nanny did it a second time. Confronted that same morning after breakfast by Dmitri, Melinda had confessed that Kasma had approached her in London and had offered her a lot of money to leave the messages and to spy on Acheron while keeping Kasma up to date with information on where they were staying. It was Melinda who had warned Dmitri that Kasma was actually on the island, news that had alarmed Acheron into making an immediate return.

The fountain of questions concerning Kasma that had disturbed Tabby earlier in the day was, by that stage, returning fast, but the haunted look in Acheron's lustrous dark eyes and the bleak set of his bronzed face silenced her. He escorted her out to a car, and she slid in, appreciating the air-conditioned cool on her overheated skin.

'I have a lot to explain,' Acheron acknowledged flatly and then he closed his hand over hers.

In a reflexive movement, Tabby rejected the contact and folded her hands together on her lap. 'After the way you behaved that last night and the fact that you haven't been in touch since, I think holding hands would be a bit of a joke,' she said bluntly. 'You don't need to pretend things you don't feel to pacify or comfort me. As you noted, I'm unhurt. It's been a horrible day but I'll get over it without leaning on you.'

'Maybe I want you to lean on me.'

Tabby raised a brow, unimpressed by that unlikely suggestion. 'I'd prefer to fall over and pick myself up. I've been doing it all my life and I've managed just fine.'

Acheron compressed his wide, sensual mouth. 'I should have explained about her weeks ago but the subject of Kasma rouses a lot of bad memories...and reactions,' he admitted with curt reluctance.

'Kasma's the reason you thought someone might have pushed me down the stairs at the villa,' Tabby grasped finally.

'Maybe she made me a little paranoid but she did destroy my relationship with my father before he died.'

'And that's why he wrote that crazy will,' Tabby guessed.

'I told you that I only met my father's family about eighteen months ago. I only agreed in the first place because it seemed to mean so much to him. What I didn't mention before is that the week before that dinner engagement took place at his home, I met Kasma *without* knowing I was meeting Kasma,' he told her grittily.

Tabby frowned. 'Without knowing it was her?' she echoed. 'How? I mean, *why*?'

'I doubt if I could *ever* adequately explain why from Kasma's point of view. She introduced herself to me as Ariadne. She certainly knew who I was,' he delivered with perceptible bitterness. 'I was in Paris on a stopover between flights and she was staying in the same hotel. I've never believed that was a coincidence. I believe I was set up. I was alone. I was bored. She targeted me and I fell for it…and you could not begin to understand how deeply I regret taking the bait.'

Tabby was studying him with confused eyes. 'The bait?'

'I had a tacky one-night stand with her,' Acheron ground out grudgingly, dark colour accentuating his spectacular cheekbones, his jaw line clenching hard on the admission. 'A couple of stolen hours from a busy schedule of work and travel. I'm being honest here—it meant nothing more to me. Although I treated her with respect I never pretended at any stage that I wanted to see her again.'

Tabby averted her eyes, reflecting that respectful treatment would not have compensated Kasma for his ultimate rejection, when presumably she had persuaded herself that she could expect a much keener and less fleeting response.

'She picked me up in the hotel restaurant. Afterwards she started acting as though she knew me really well. To be frank, it was a freaky experience and I made my excuses and returned to my own room.'

Tabby was swallowing hard at a level of honesty she had not expected to receive from him. 'But if she already knew who you were, why did she lie about her own identity?'

Acheron shrugged a broad shoulder. 'Obviously because I would never have touched her had I known she was my father's precious little girl.'

'His precious little girl?' Tabby queried.

'Her mother was widowed when Kasma was only a baby. My father raised Kasma from the age of three. She was the apple of his eye, his favourite child, and he couldn't see any fault in her,' Acheron advanced tautly, his lips compressing. 'When I walked into the family dinner the week after the hotel encounter I was appalled to realise that Kasma was my father's stepchild and furious that she had lied to me and put me in that position, but that wasn't all I had to worry about. Before I could even decide how to behave, she stood up and announced that she had been saving a little surprise for everyone. And that surprise—according to her—was that she and I were *dating*.'

'Oh, my word…' Tabby was as stunned as he must've been by that development. 'And that one…er…episode at the hotel was really the extent of your relationship with her?'

'It was, but not according to Kasma. She had a very fertile imagination and over the months that followed she began acting like a stalker, flying round the world, turning up wherever I was,' he explained, lines of strain bracketing his mouth as he recalled that period. 'She tried to force her way into my life while telling my father a pack of lies about me. She told him I'd cheated on her, she told him I'd got her pregnant and then she told him she'd had a miscarriage. He fell for every one of her tales and nothing I could say would persuade him that my relationship with his stepdaughter was a fantasy she had made up. And having made that first mistake by getting involved with her that night at the hotel, I felt I had brought the whole nightmare down on my own head.'

'I don't think so—'

'It was casual sex but there was nothing casual about it,' Acheron opined grimly. 'I went to bed with a woman who was a stranger and maybe I deserved what I got.'

'Not when she set out to deliberately deceive you and then tried to trap you into a relationship,' Tabby declared stoutly. 'I don't agree with the way you behaved with her but she was obviously a disturbed personality.'

'She assaulted a woman I spent time with last year, which was why I was so concerned about your safety and Amber's.'

'What did she do?'

'She forced her way into my apartment and punched the woman while ranting about how I belonged to her.' He grimaced at the recollection. 'My father begged me to use my influence and prevent it from going to court but I was at the end of my rope. Kasma was dangerous and she needed treatment but as long as her family turned a blind eye and I swallowed what she was dishing out, she was free to do as she liked. The court accepted that she was lying and had never had a relationship with me and therefore had no excuse whatsoever for attacking the woman in my apartment and calling it a domestic dispute.'

'Didn't that convince your father that you were telling him the truth?'

'No, Kasma managed to convince him that I must've bribed someone and she had been stitched up by me to protect my own reputation,' he proffered with unconcealed regret. 'The sole saving grace was that after that court case I was able to take out a restraining order against her and at least that kept her out of my hair while I was on Greek soil.'

Tabby slowly shook her head, which was reeling with his revelations. 'Why didn't you tell me about her? Why wouldn't you explain?'

His bold bronzed profile clenched hard. 'I was ashamed of the whole business and I didn't want to frighten you either. My wealth didn't protect me from the fact that Kasma could still get to me almost everywhere I went. You have no idea how powerless I felt when she even managed to gatecrash the wedding because I didn't want to make a scene with my father's family present,' he confessed grittily. 'I didn't want to publicise my problems with her while my father was still alive either. She caused him enough grief with her wild stories about how badly I'd treated her.'

'So why on earth did he want you to marry her?' Tabby queried, struggling to understand that angle.

'He believed she loved me and he genuinely thought I owed her a wedding ring. He blamed me for her increasingly hysterical outbursts and strange behaviour.'

'That was probably easier for him than dealing with the real problem, which was *her*. He would've had more faith in you if he had ever had the chance to get to know you properly,' Tabby opined, resting a soothing hand down on his. 'Kasma had the advantage and he trusted her and that gave her the power to put you through an awful ordeal.'

'It's over now,' Acheron reminded her flatly. 'Her brother, Simeon, believed me and tried to persuade her to see a therapist. Perhaps if she had listened she might not have died today.'

'It's not your fault though,' Tabby countered steadily. 'You weren't capable of fixing whatever was broken in her.'

Acheron groaned out loud. 'It's so *not* sexy that you feel sorry for me now.'

'I don't feel sorry for you. I just think you've been put through the mill a bit,' Tabby paraphrased awkwardly. 'No wonder you don't like clingy, needy women after that experience.'

'I wouldn't mind if you clung occasionally,' Acheron admitted.

Tabby rolled her eyes at him. 'Stop being such a smoothie…it's wasted on me.'

'What do you mean?' Acheron asked harshly as the limo drew up outside the beach house.

'It's not necessary to charm me. We both had good reasons to get married and that's the only fulfilment either of us require from our agreement. You got a wife and, hopefully, I will eventually be able to adopt Amber,' Tabby spelt out as she slid out of the car and walked into the house.

'That's not how I feel,' Acheron informed her stubbornly.

'We're not twin souls and nor are we required to be,' Tabby flipped back, walking through to the lounge, which stood with doors wide open to the terrace and the view of the cove, draperies fluttering softly in the slight breeze that never seemed to leave the coast. 'I think we're overdue a little plain speaking here.'

Outside, she leant up against the rail bordering the terrace and folded her arms in a defensive position. She knew what she needed to say. She was more than halfway to getting her heart broken by the stupid, dangerous pretence that she was on a *real* honeymoon with a *real* husband! How had she let that happen? How had she let herself fall in love with a male who was simply doing what he had to do to give the appearance of being a newly married man?

'Meaning?' Acheron prompted, stilling in the doorway, six feet plus inches of stunning male beauty and charisma.

Tabby looked him over with carefully blank eyes. He was gorgeous; he had always been gorgeous from the crown of his slightly curly black head to the soles of his equally perfect feet. He focused sizzling dark golden eyes on her with interrogative intensity.

'Tabby?' he prompted afresh.

'Unlike you I call a spade a spade. I don't wrap it up.'

'I appreciate that about you...that what you say you mean,' he countered steadily.

Tabby threw her slight shoulders back, violet eyes wide and appealing. 'Look, let's just bring the whole charade to an end here and now,' she urged. 'Melinda was spying on us and she's gone. We've done all the newly happily married stuff for weeks and now surely we can both go back to normal?'

'Normal?'

Tabby was wondering what the matter with him was, for it was not like him to take a back seat in any argument. Furthermore, he looked strained, having lost colour while his spectacular strong bone structure had set rigid below his bronzed skin. 'We were strangers with a legal agreement, Ash,' she reminded him painfully. 'We've met the terms, put on the show and now surely we can return to being ourselves again behind closed doors at least?'

'Is that what you want?' he pressed curtly, lean brown hands closing into fists by his side. 'Don't you think this is a decision best shelved for a less traumatic day?'

Tabby lifted her chin, her heart squeezing tight inside her chest, pain like a sharp little arrow twisting inside her because, of course, it was not what she wanted. She wanted him; she was in love with him but she had to protect herself, had to force herself to accept that what they had shared was only a pretence. 'No.'

'You want to go back to where we started out?' Acheron demanded starkly.

Tabby dropped her shoulders, her eyes veiling. 'No, I just want us to be honest and not faking anything.'

Acheron breathed in very slow and deep, dark golden eyes glittering like fireworks below the shield of his luxuriant black lashes. 'I *haven't* been faking anything...'

Tabby's dazed mind ran over all the romancing, the sexing, the hand-holding, the fun, and she blinked in bemusement. 'But *of course* you were faking.'

'It may have started out that way, but it ended up real, *yineka mou.*' Acheron surveyed her steadily but she knew he was putting up a front because he was really, really tense.

'How…*real*?' Tabby questioned, her heart thumping like mad.

Acheron lifted his arms and spread his hands in an oddly defenceless gesture. 'I fell in love with you…'

Tabby almost fell over in shock, her brain refusing to accept that he could have said that he loved her. 'I don't believe you. You're just scared that I'm about to walk out on our marriage agreement and you'll lose your company—but you don't *need* to be scared of that happening because I wouldn't do that to you. I'm still as determined to adopt Amber as I ever was, so I couldn't do that even if I wanted to,' she pointed out honestly.

'When I try to say, "I love you" for the first time in my life to a woman, you could at least listen to what I'm saying and stop talking a lot of rubbish!' Acheron shot back at her with scorching effect.

Tabby was struck dumb by that little speech. He was serious? He wasn't joking, faking, trying to manipulate her in some nefarious way? She stared back at him fixedly.

'And it was bloody hard to say too!' Acheron added in angry complaint at her response.

'I'm in shock,' Tabby mumbled shakily. 'I didn't think you had any feelings for me.'

'I tried very hard not to. I fought it every step of the way,' Acheron admitted ruefully. 'But in the end you got to me and you got to me so hard I ran away from it.'

'Ran away?' Tabby almost whispered in growing disbelief.

'I was feeling strange and that's why I took off on business…to give myself a little breathing space,' Acheron qualified tautly. 'But the minute I got away I realised I only wanted to come back and be with you.'

Tabby blinked slowly, struggling to react to that explanation when all her crazy head was full of was a single statement: that he loved her. *He loves me*. She tasted the idea, savoured it, very nearly careened across the terrace and flattened him to the tiles in gratitude, but mercifully retained enough restraint to stay where she was. 'You got cold feet, didn't you?' she guessed.

Acheron nodded. 'It was a little overwhelming when I realised what was wrong with me.'

Tabby moved closer. 'No, it wasn't anything wrong with you. It was a good thing, a wonderful thing...you love me. I love you.'

'If you feel the same way I do, why the hell are you putting me through this torture?' Acheron demanded rawly.

Tabby almost laughed, a sense of intoxication gripping her as she searched his darkly handsome features and the masculine bewilderment etched there. 'Talking about love is torture?'

Acheron rested his arms down on her slim shoulders and breathed, 'I thought once I said it, that would be that, but I was scared you wouldn't feel the same way and that you wanted it all to be fake.'

Tabby closed her arms round him and snuggled

close. 'No, real is much better than fake. So, does this mean we're really and truly married?'

'Absolutely,' Acheron confirmed, and bent to lift her up into his arms. 'It also means we're going to be adoptive parents together because I sort of developed a fondness for Amber as well. Seems this love business is contagious...'

'Wow...' Tabby framed as he carried her upstairs to their bedroom and Teresa, with the baby in her arms, retreated back into the nursery with a warm smile. 'But how did it happen?'

Acheron arranged her on the bed with the care of a man setting up an art installation and stared down at her for what felt like ages. 'I think it started when I realised I was with a woman who was willing to sacrifice her home and her business to look after her sick best friend and child. I respect that level of loyalty and unselfishness. I respect what you were willing to do to retain custody of Amber even though I was pretty rough and crude about everything at the time. You stuck it out...you stood up to me...'

'And out of that came love?' Tabby whispered in shock.

'Out of those experiences came a woman I couldn't live without,' traded Acheron with a tender look in his lustrous dark eyes that she had never seen before. '*Thee mou*...if you had still wanted the fake marriage and the divorce I don't know what I would've done.'

'I don't want a divorce...I don't ever want to let go of you,' Tabby confided against his shirtfront.

'That desire is just about to come in very handy, *agape mou*,' Acheron murmured thickly, claiming her ripe mouth with his own, sending a thrill of heat and anticipation travelling through her relaxed body.

About an hour later, Acheron leapt naked out of bed to retrieve his trousers and dig into a pocket to produce a jewellers' box, which he pressed into her hand. 'I know it's not your birthday for another twenty-four hours but this is burning a hole in my pocket,' he admitted ruefully.

Tabby opened the box to find an unusual ring in the shape of a rose with a ruby at the centre.

'What do you think?' Acheron demanded anxiously. 'I wanted you to know that it was made in the image of your tattoo because it will always remind me what made you the special woman you are.'

'It's…gorgeous!' Tabby carolled as he removed his late mother's engagement ring from her wedding finger and replaced it with the new ring. The diamonds on the rose petals caught the sunlight and cast a rainbow of little sparkling reflections across the white bedding. 'But why on earth do you think I am so special when I'm so ordinary?'

'You're special because in spite of all the bad things that happened to you, you still have an open heart and a loving spirit. You love Amber, you love me—'

'So much,' Tabby emphasised feelingly as she smiled up at him. 'Although you might feel you love me a little less when you see what I spent on my credit card.'

'Never,' Acheron contradicted. 'You're the least extravagant person I know.'

'You might change your mind on that score,' she warned him, hoping he at least appreciated the gift of the pen on his birthday in three days' time.

'I love you,' he breathed softly, his attention locked on her smiling face.

He had fallen in love with her, he had genuinely fallen in love with her, Tabby savoured finally, and she allowed the happiness to well up inside her along with a sense of release from all anxiety. Somehow, by the most mysterious process of love known to mankind, two people who had loathed each other on sight because of their misconceptions had found love and formed a happy home and family and she was delirious with the joy of that miracle.

Tabby sucked in her tummy and studied the mirror. No, it was pointless: she was pregnant and there was no escaping that pregnant apple shape, no matter how well cut her maternity clothing was. With a wry smile at the foolishness of her vanity, Tabby went downstairs to check the last-minute arrangements for Amber's fourth birthday party.

The party was a catered affair, everything set up to entertain a whole posse of Amber's nursery-school friends. There was a bouncy castle in the garden of their London town house, purchased after the birth of their first child, Andreus, who was already a rumbustious noisy toddler. Closely pursued by his nanny, Teresa, who had become as much a part of the family as the children, Andreus hurtled across the hall to throw his arms up to be lifted by his mother.

Tabby tried not to wince at the weight of her son, but, at eight months along in her second pregnancy, lifting a child who was already outstripping his peers in size was becoming quite a challenge. He hugged her tight, black curls like his father's silky against her throat, her own big blue eyes bright in his little smiling face. Sometimes, Tabby was still afraid that if she blinked her happy family life would disappear and she would discover she had been trapped in an inordinately convincing and wonderful daydream. And then she would look at Acheron and the children and she would be soothed by the closeness of their bonds.

Admittedly she would never have picked Acheron out as a keen father figure when she first met him, but exposure to Amber's charms had soon raised a desire in Acheron to have a child of his own. By the time the legalities of Amber's adoption had been settled and she had officially become their daughter, Tabby had been expecting Andreus. The little girl whom Tabby was currently carrying had been more of an accidental conception, thanks to a little spur-of-the-moment lovemaking on the beach in Sardinia where they had first found love, and which of all Acheron's properties they visited the most, although they had quickly extended the house to add on more bedroom capacity.

His father's widow, Ianthe, and her two surviving children had stayed with them there to attend Kasma's funeral. It had been a sad and sobering occasion but it had also done much to build a bridge between Ash and his father's former family. Ianthe had admitted to having been seriously worried about her daughter's mental health but Ash's late father, Angelos, had refused to face up to that reality. Kasma's brother, Simeon, and his family also had young children and the two couples had become close friends since that last sad encounter.

The front door opened and Andreus scrambled down from his mother's arms to hurl himself violently at Acheron, shouting, 'Dad!' at the top of his voice.

Tabby watched Acheron scoop his son up, and a warm smile curved her generous mouth because she never loved Acheron more than when she saw him with the children. He was kind, affectionate and patient, all the things that they had both so badly lacked when they were kids themselves. 'I thought you wouldn't make it back in time.'

'Where's the birthday girl?' Acheron enquired.

Amber came racing downstairs, a vivid little figure clad in a flouncy new party dress, and flung herself at her father with very little more circumspection than her toddler brother. 'You're here!' she carolled. 'You're here for my party.'

'Of course, I am,' Acheron said in the act of producing a present from behind his back, only to laugh as the housekeeper opened the door to let Amber's best friend and her mother enter and the two little girls went running off together. 'So much for being flavour of the month there!' he teased.

'But you're always my favourite flavour,' Tabby rushed to assure him in an undertone before she went to greet the arriving guests.

Acheron watched her acting hostess with quiet admiration. *His* Tabby, the best and luckiest find he had ever made, always warm, sunny and bright and still the most loving creature he had ever met. It didn't surprise him in the slightest that he loved her more with every passing year.

* * * * *

OKANAGAN REGIONAL LIBRARY
3 3132 03644 4430